Cobalt City:
Ties that Bind

Written by Nathan Crowder

CONTENTS

The De La Vega Mysteries
Greetings from Buena Rosa
Ride Like the Devil

The Protectorate Series
Chanson Noir
Cobalt City Blues

Other Cobalt City Books by Nathan Crowder

Cobalt City: Los Muertos
Cobalt City: Ties That Bind
Cobalt City: Resistance

Cobalt City Anthologies Edited by Nathan Crowder

Cobalt City Christmas
Cobalt City Christmas: Christmas Harder
Cobalt City Dark Carnival
Cobalt City Timeslip

CHAPTER ONE—VELVET

All things being equal, I'd rather be gnawed on by that Russian bear crime boss again than suffer through another boring society function. But this one was being held at Tessien's, one of Parkside's finer dining establishments, and I was a sucker for their crab cakes. Otherwise, I might have skipped the benefit for whatever endangered animal the Cobalt City society crowd was enamored with this particular week. Big display boards showing a small pig-like animal, brown with white stripes down his back, were propped on easels behind an information table along the far wall. It looked out of place amidst the candlelight, polished glass and black wood, and long white drapes. It felt like we were holding some kind of metropolitan funeral or a strangely upscale science fair. If I really wanted to know the animal's name, I'd go read the pamphlets, but a minefield of annoying people stretched between me the information table. The silver chafing dishes laden with crab cakes and assorted hors d'oeuvres were closer, so I held my ground with the annoying people at my table instead.

I'm not here for that social scene bullshit. I'm just here for the crab cakes.

It was a lie, of course. I'd gotten a lot of mileage in years past lying to myself. I was a pro. It wasn't that I didn't care about endangered animals. On the long list of things wrong with this world, adorable piggies were not my highest priority. But I wasn't here just for the crab cakes, even if it was the food that got me out the door. My life is just ... complicated. I had come to a place in my life where it was now necessary to put on appearances, to remind people that society darling and former wild child Julianna Vanderkamp was still alive. The society crowd had, at best, a schizophrenic memory—quick to remember embarrassing details,

1

quicker still to forget people they judged past their expiration date. I'd been so busy with other matters lately, I'm frankly surprised the country club hadn't put my face on a milk carton yet.

I had a lot of loose contacts in this crowd. People who used to be friends. I cut back after my party girl ways almost killed me a few years ago. Cut *way* back. Boring functions like this kept me on the radar—kept tenuous social ties from atrophying completely. I couldn't let people forget about me any more than I could have them begin speculating what I'd been up to lately.

I locked my polite smile in place like a mask while half paying attention to talk of yachting at my table. It was a sultry July evening. The air conditioner was doing valiant battle with the outside temperatures, but it did nothing to dull the olfactory cocktail of socialites who didn't know how to exercise restraint with their perfume. I was distracted by the thought of my father's yacht in Cape Cod. It had been at least a year since I had gone sailing with my dad on the *Coriander*. The salt air and cool sunset breeze had mixed poorly with the stilted, awkward conversation about what I was doing with my life, which was, in his eyes, nothing.

Despite the lackluster conversations and Chanel assault at Tessien's, at least I didn't have to do the "you're wasting your life" dance here. No one in the society crowd cared too much about what I was doing with my life. Everything was surface. Everything was small talk and putting on appearances. As long as the veneer didn't crack, no one saw beneath the surface.

No one would have to talk about how this lifestyle almost killed me.

No one probed deeply enough that I'd have to lie about being a superhero.

"We really haven't seen much of you since—" Vikki's smile faltered for a second before she managed to come up with a side-step around difficult truths. "Well, since the incident. We should get the girls together for brunch soon!"

Either Vikki had a hard time letting go, or she had no concept of the passage of time. We'd gone to school together a decade ago before departing for different universities. I'd changed and she hadn't. Even the lightly curled black hair that framed her carefully tanned face was the same cut as it had always been.

I wasn't feeling the same nostalgia. Vikki had been there on the rooftop deck of the Jaguar Club that night three years ago. She'd watched as three of us took a cocktail of pills and booze that would have given Jim Morrison pause. Chase Hammond had died, and Abigail Walton was still in a coma. I wondered which "girls" Vikki intended to get together for brunch. Other than the two of us, the only one left from that night was Denise, who had left the city soon after, severing all contact. A friend of a friend told me she lived in Wyoming now. I also wondered if ... no, *when* Abby woke up from her coma if she'd have superpowers like me.

"That would be nice," I lied. "Drop me a text sometime and we'll try and set up a Sunday."

I turned my attention back to the crab cakes with that delicious drizzle of aioli. Focusing on my plate was better than the other option: getting dragged into casual conversation with the other five people at the table. Starting with Vikki who sat to my left, there was her date, who looked vaguely familiar; another old classmate named Graham Caulfield, who I always strongly disliked; his date, Natalie, who I'd never seen before but who seemed overeager to make Graham happy; and Marlene Chambers, who was a sweet if clueless society matron in her late fifties. I tuned them out. It wasn't so much a superpower as a carefully developed skill.

I was dragged me back into the conversation by Graham's icy scalpel of a voice and the awkward silence that followed. "No one asked what you think."

I glanced around the table, seeing all eyes turned not on Graham but on Natalie. She had recoiled like a scolded pup, stunned blinking as she leaned back in her chair. A smile fluttered on her youthful face, a butterfly in a hurricane. "I'm sorry."

Graham's sneer of victory was far too familiar. He'd been an enormous asshole back at Cabot Academy, the Regency Heights private school responsible for most of the people in this room. Not much about Graham had changed other than thirty extra pounds and thinner hair. But he had money, and with that came certain perks. Like being able to treat people like crap. Like a sense of entitlement where he gave orders and expect them to be followed. At Cabot, he had been fixated on a girl in our class. I couldn't remember her name. Graham pursued her relentlessly until he finally wore her down. They dated a few weeks until he got bored and moved on. Or she had moved away. I couldn't remember, really. It wasn't like we were friends.

A better person would have tried to warn that half-remembered girl away from Graham. But I hadn't been a good person then. I had even torn her down once or twice. Casually, and not with malicious intent. Since then, I had come to realize in so many ways that had been much worse. I had lost sleep since "the incident," wondering if I would still be that bad person if not for such a dramatic wake-up call.

Surviving the overdose changed my perspective, gave me a purpose and direction that I'd been lacking. It also gave me the strength to crush cinderblocks in my hand and jump higher than any of the skyscrapers in Cobalt City. It even sharpened up my brain meats as part of the package. I gave up the party girl life to become a hero. Julianna Vanderkamp had been, at times at least, an entitled, self-focused bitch, so I retired her. I put my focus on being Velvet instead.

I wished I could remember the name of Graham's ex-girlfriend. I told myself if I could remember her name, it would make me feel better about how I acted then. But I couldn't. So it didn't.

I'd dealt with a lot of professional-grade creeps in the past few years: criminal masterminds, mad scientists, aliens from other planets and other dimensions. Graham Caulfield was every bit as slimy as them. Every bit as unsettling. Maybe it was because I'd seen his particular flavor of ingrained casual cruelty first hand. Maybe it was because I was more familiar with it.

If he was more ambitious, I could easily see him as one more villain ready to be smote. It was unfortunate I had to share a table with him. I couldn't imagine why someone like Natalie would want to date him.

I didn't know her, but his rebuke and her reaction to it made me curious. This party was boring, but at least this little mystery had me engaged. It should go without saying that nothing good has ever come from me being bored.

Natalie seemed sweet enough. Polite. Reasonably smart when she did dare to speak. Her laugh was light and a bit fragile. She was younger than anyone else at the table, but her exact age was difficult to pinpoint. She could have been sixteen or maybe as old as early twenties, but no older, though there was an unmistakable maturity in her eyes. This was a girl who had seen some shit.

4

And there was the way Natalie kept a close eye on her date, constantly aware of his mood, his approval, eager to please.

I couldn't put my finger on that look in her eyes. But I sure as fuck knew it wasn't love.

Poor girl.

"I heard Pin is back in town," Vikki said breathlessly.

I tried not to roll my eyes. I'd grown up with this in Cobalt City—this ongoing gossip and speculation over the comings and goings of the cape and cowl crowd. The heroes were constant, reassuring like oatmeal, while the villains like Pin always seemed to be the more exciting topics, like a flaming dessert of some kind. Pin was a morbid curiosity, an object lesson, maybe, a failed shock rocker named Craig Bushnell who became a murderer to compensate for his lack of artistic talent.

I'd also known he was back in town before anyone at my table.

As part of the Protectorate, I'd been one of the first on the scene two days ago when he abducted his newest victims. "I heard that Velvet, Worm Queen, and Knockabout had already stomped a mud-hole in his ass," I glanced at Ms. Chambers, having forgotten for a moment that I was in a more formal setting. "Sorry for my language."

Marlene Chambers chuckled dryly, "That leather-clad attention whore had it coming. I hope Velvet tore his balls off. If he has any."

Natalie got half a laugh out before a sharp look from Graham cut her off. Ok, so laughing at crude old ladies was not approved, ladylike behavior, apparently.

Being careful not to say more than I could have read in the papers, I shrugged. "I kind of hope she did, too." Though I knew that she—I—hadn't. We had administered a beat-down, but the primary goal was to rescue the five potential victims before Pin did something "artistic" to them. The hardcore nutcase had managed to escape. If I was more of the investigation type, I'd be out there looking for him right now. But I know my strengths, and the strengths of the rest of the Protectorate. Between the analytical genius of Archon, and the finely honed hunting instincts of Wild Kat and Huntsman, they'd have Pin tracked down soon enough.

My brain was sharper before, but it didn't help me out there. If they needed someone who could punch through a truck, they knew where to find me.

"So, Natalie," I ventured as casually as possible. "Where did you meet our Graham?"

She froze, but only for a few seconds before Graham fielded the question himself. His hand was below the table, squeezing her hand in reassurance, I wondered, or warning?

"We were introduced by mutual friends," Graham said. He looked to Natalie for confirmation and she nodded slightly. Composed.

No. Not composed. Controlled.

I pushed, I realized, not because of any protective instinct for Natalie who I didn't know, but out of dislike for Graham. "Oh? Anyone I would know?"

"I wish!" His smile was a wolf's smile. Genuine but hungry, laughing at a joke he wouldn't share.

God ... I do not miss seeing him around.

Natalie leaned over to whisper something into Graham's ear. His smile did not falter, his gaze did not turn from me, but I watched it slide from my face to the plunging neckline of my silver-sequined Manu Julien gown. After a few seconds, he transferred his napkin from lap to plate. "If you'll excuse us."

As they walked from the table toward the bar, I wondered if anyone else noticed that Graham held his date's wrist in a vise-like grip. Vikki's date, who had hardly said a complete sentence all evening, smiled, oblivious, and said, "They seemed nice."

Vikki looked down at her plate, her voice carefully neutral to not to sound contradictory. "Same old Graham." She reached for her drink to wash the taste of his name from her mouth, no doubt.

"A lot like his father," Ms. Chambers said. "For better or worse. But the girl seems nice. Maybe she'll soothe his temperament a bit. Maybe not."

I wanted to ask more. The sullen silence Ms. Chambers sank into suggested she knew more than she was letting on. And as much as I disliked Graham Caulfield, the opportunity to get some dirt on him and his family appealed to my baser instincts. I put it down to the old Julianna Vanderkamp, the one who lived and died by gossip. That wasn't who I was anymore, as further evidenced by the vibrations coming from the little silver clutch purse on the table near my left hand.

I snapped it open to remove my phone with an apologetic smile. I knew it was a breach of social protocol to check my cell phone at a time like this, but call me a rebel. As I opened the text from the Protectorate, I really hoped it was a call to action because Pin had been found. The idea of smashing his smug face once or twice filled me with an undue amount of satisfaction.

No such luck on Pin. But at least the text promised a bit of action.

Metahuman assassin and unknown cape involved in firefight. Civilians in line of fire. Cooke Hotel.

The Cooke was close by, a faded but once grand hotel that coasted by on reputation more than amenities. I texted back, "2 minutes," before pushing back from the table.

Vikki gave me a bit of a dismayed look at the prospect of being left behind with her date and Marlene, trying to make conversation. "You're going?"

"Yep! The new guy needs some ... attention," I said, knowing Vikki would excuse a booty call, though my dating life these days was even thinner than my excuse to bail. "Call me. We'll do brunch!" I smiled cheerily as I waved goodbye, already planning an excuse to cancel on brunch.

I slipped out the front and rounded the corner into the thankfully vacant alley. Tessien's was on the ground floor of a twenty floor luxury condo development. I bounded to the rooftop without hesitation, sighted on the roofline of my building three blocks away and leapt to it with only the slightest grunt of exertion. I dropped onto my penthouse deck on the far side of the roof and slipped through the sliding glass doors into the tastefully appointed living room.

The giant Charles Heyen original, a batik piece depicting three slender, brightly colored men in abstract, moved aside with a soft click to reveal my costume locker. I let my gown hit the floor and replaced it with my short blue uniform dress. I snapped the bulky utility belt in place, adjusting its weight across the top of my hips. I dropped the boots on the ground and stepped into them, feeling them cinch in place with my weight on the internal pressure sensors. I tossed on and secured the midnight blue bullet-proof cape and hood. Finally, the elbow length gauntlets, like an iron glove wrapped in velvet. All the finest money could design and pay for.

Here's the thing about privilege that I was constantly re-learning: when you have it, it's real easy to not see it. Most of the people in Tessien's had money like I did, but how many of them used it to do something? The sad answer, none of them. Because they tended not to think very far outside of their own circumstances. I'd been there. It took a massive shock to my system to open my eyes. I'd been a spoiled rich kid my entire life. Mom and Dad had a big estate across the river in Regency Heights. I got an expensive degree in Economics without learning a single damn thing about economics. As rarely as I attended class, I suspected the reason I got a diploma at all was due to a whole other kind of economics. Not that I cared at the time. It wasn't my money, and it wasn't my problem.

I was a fuckup who had never looked beyond the next party, beyond what would make me happy in the moment. I didn't care about anyone unless they could do something for me.

Then a bunch of us girls rolled the dice on some unknown street drugs at a party at some weirdly Aztec-themed club that was long since closed. I survived, after a fashion. But the person I had been was as good as dead. There's nothing like staring down the barrel of a final sleep to make a girl take stock of their life, their impact in the world.

I got a second chance, and the power to do something with it. So I decided to make a different impact and use my resources to fund my exploits as Velvet.

I thought again of Graham leading Natalie away by the wrist. He had been angry. I knew him well enough to know that. And my prying questions had been at least partly to blame. My stomach tightened at the thought. *I hope Natalie is okay.* She seemed nice. But even if she wasn't exactly nice, she didn't deserve Graham's anger. No one deserved that.

I pushed the thought away. It wouldn't do me any good now.

With twenty seconds to spare, I launched from my patio toward the Cooke Hotel eight blocks away, eager for a problem I could punch.

8

CHAPTER TWO—BANTAM

If you keep your ear to the street like I do, you tend to hear things. For instance, I heard about group of hero nerds who created a complicated ranking system of all known capes, whether they're heroes or villains or those like me who sort of fall in-between. They evolved this into online message boards and, believe it or not, a sort of fantasy league. I clean up on my office fantasy basketball pool, but this was a kind of alchemy beyond even me. My activity on the fringes of the Cobalt City cape and cowl scene proved to be little to no help. But even if I wasn't going to win any tournaments, I found their system of defining the relative "weight class" of given super powered individuals fascinating.

I was stunned to see that even I was ranked on their boards. I thought I was being discreet. Or at least as discreet as a vigilante in a rooster mask could be in this town. Apparently I wasn't discreet enough, because there I was, sixth from the bottom. To be fair, in addition to being new, I hadn't displayed any powers, just a pair of tonfa fighting batons, toe-spurs on my boots, and compact glider wings built into my costume. It made sense that I'd be feather weight. Bantam weight, if you will. The only capes ranked lower were ones I tended to think of as jokes or tourists who were going to get themselves killed wearing spandex. Snowflake, the panda who flew the plane for the Protectorate, ranked above me.

I'll admit, I was kind of hurt by that at first. But I had to be honest with myself and trust the geeks with their system. Knockabout could stop an army single-handedly. Mister Grey was a terrifying, immortal cloud of crematorium ash in human form. I could beat on a fool with my sticks. The rankings hurt, but not as much as having my spine ripped out by over-estimating my own abilities in a very rough town.

I joined the cape fantasy league and was slowly figuring out the system. I made a point not to draft myself, as I felt that would be unethical, especially after the corruption scandal that hit the Cobalt City Blue Blazers last season. In addition to keeping me occupied with another fantasy league, I used it as a guide to make informed decisions. When I pulled on the stylized rooster mask, I made it a habit not to pick fights outside of my weight class.

I don't know what kind of medical plans other Cobalt City heroes might have, but I was stuck on the police department's plan. If I showed up at my HMO with a proton blast wound, questions were going to be asked. The more questions I could avoid, the happier I'd be.

Bad enough I had a dead dad with a criminal record. Bad enough that I wasn't white, and a woman to boot, and barely met the department's height guidelines at 5' 7". Bad enough I didn't play well with others and hadn't been assigned a partner since Olson transferred to vice in January. If word leaked that I put on a mask to do things as Bantam that I couldn't do as a cop, I'd be out of a job. I'd be lucky to not end up in jail.

I learned to embrace anonymity. You hear of people like Stardust or Velvet or even Gato Loco because the press loves the glamour of people in costumes stopping other people in costumes from committing crime. I vowed to keep it simple—to keep under the radar. No capes. If they had a costume or powers or a name like "Dr. Destruction" or "The Reaver," they were someone else's problem.

I didn't need press clippings to feel like I was making a difference. I didn't need to climb the ranks in the fantasy league. There was still plenty of crime in Cobalt City committed by ordinary people making very bad decisions. No, it wasn't glamorous. But even without costumes or powers, they were real monsters. They didn't bother to wear masks because their victims were their own family, their neighbors. So I was able to work in the shadows because acknowledging me meant admitting that a person doesn't need a death ray and an iron mask to be evil. No one wants to read that over their morning coffee

When I heard that there was someone with a gun spotted entering an old hotel practically around the corner from me, I figured it wouldn't hurt to check. Give me a guy with a gun over some psycho with telepathic wolves any day of the week. He was relatively easy to spot, too. It was as hot and muggy as Satan's taint, and this joker was wearing a trench coat.

In retrospect, that should have been a red flag.

I didn't recognize the fucker until he pulled on his mask. He was distinctive with the mask: a black full-head affair with a giant blue circle over the face. A contract killer, new to the Cobalt City scene, he signed his two kills as "Regret." The reports I'd read said he carried two custom guns that fired a variety of specialized ammunition, which he proved to be true by whipping them out in the hotel lobby. At that point, it was kind of too late for me to change my mind.

As the two midnight-black hand-cannons appeared from under his trench coat, I scanned for his potential targets. Despite my rooster mask, he hadn't seemed to really notice me yet, and trained killer or not, he telegraphed his targets like a goddamned amateur. He had sighted on two people stepping out of the fancy hotel bar across the lobby, a man and woman in their fifties, both white, both distinctly middle-class—not the kinds of people one usually pictured as the targets for a paid assassin. What could they have possibly done except maybe let the front lawn get a bit out of control? But in my years in Cobalt City, I'd seen people killed for less. And here I was, the only person available to stop a contract killer from collecting his paycheck.

There was no time to think, not even to second-guess myself. I launched a flying kick straight into Regret's kidney. The impact was enough to knock him over, and the toe-spur in my boot sliced through his coat. He tumbled across the worn gold-flecked maroon of the lobby carpet and came up in a crouch facing me, no worse for wear. It gave me the first good look at what he was wearing under the coat.

Kevlar body armor. Shit. That's the last goddamned thing I need right now.

I had my tonfa out, the length of each club down my forearms, ready to block. But two guns beats two sticks, especially with fifteen feet between us. I told myself that at least I bought the intended targets some time, but both of them had frozen up next to this potted plant, a big bastard with wide, deep green leaves that looked more at home in a jungle than a hotel lobby in New England. So much for hoping the rabbits would run.

11

"I don't know who you are," Regret said, "But you'll bleed like the rest."

Several years on the force and even more growing up in my dad's shadow taught me the sound of a guy putting on a fake tough-guy voice. Despite the Kevlar, mask, guns, and stated occupation on his theoretical business card, this guy was not the world-class bad-ass he liked to project himself to be. I was pretty certain he'd never squared up against another cape in his life. That said, he was still a confirmed killer with specialized gun, body armor, and the benefit of range on me.

He was out of my weight class. No doubt about it. FantasyCape.com would probably have given me long odds on dropping him. 25-to-1 was my guess. He opened up on me with one of his guns, and I had the good sense to recognize he wasn't just waving them around as a threat. I flipped backward and the shot passed inches below me as I got the hell out of the way. I came down on the other side of a leather sofa that looked as solid as a mid-sized sedan that had taken the bullet meant for me. The shot had dented the leather but not punctured it. Sandbag rounds. Non-lethal.

I doubted someone put him on retainer to tenderize this couple, so he might have balked at the idea of killing a cape. I might not be high profile, or any profile for that matter, but killing someone in a mask puts a very particular target on a person's back. There were far worse rounds he could have unloaded in my direction. His last kill had burned up from the inside out. While that target had been a sleazy banker connected to a billion dollar fraud scheme, immolation was still a hell of a way to go. While I could kind of appreciate him going easy on me so far, I also didn't much care for his condescension, though it may have been the only thing keeping me alive at that particular juncture.

Regret must have figured me out of the fight because he turned back toward his targets, ignoring me. I hurled one of the heavy sofa cushions at his arms with every ounce of strength I had. It might have been out of spite at being dismissed so readily, but it was enough to throw off his aim. The huge bronze-finished planter holding the jungle plant paid the ultimate sacrifice and showered the two screaming targets with dirt and ceramic dust. That was enough to get them moving, and both husband and wife, or I'm guessing husband and wife, dodged back into the hotel bar. If they couldn't find the back exit, they had just boxed themselves in, but it was still better than standing in plain sight with thumbs up their respective rectums.

It still put me no closer to stopping Regret. I could close the distance, but the likelihood of getting shot at least once was phenomenally high. I crunched the numbers in my head, a skill that would have made me a great insurance actuary had I not dreamed for something different. It was automatic, a learned response to pick out this assassin's weak points. He had his weaknesses. Everyone did. Despite the body armor on his torso and probably lighter weight armor plating on arms and legs, his joints were still relatively unprotected just to allow him freedom of motion. His mask looked lightly armored, flexible like ballistic weave, so it would stop penetration from a bullet and prevent slicing, but he would still be vulnerable to a blunt force trauma, which I could provide in spades. But seeing a weakness and being able to exploit it were two very different beasts. For me to press my advantage, I had to get within striking distance or fling my weapons at him, which was one hell of a gamble. With no practical cover between us, the chances of losing my weapon or catching a bullet were high.

He must have seen me considering making a stupid decision because he fired off two more shots in my direction to dissuade me. The first hit the sofa and froze it solid. The second filled my area with a choking smoke that forced me to pull back even farther, behind a pillar on my left.

That's when she showed up.

I had seen Velvet in the news for a while now, first attached to Starcom innovator Jaccob Stevens as something of a troubleshooter, and then as a member of the local superhero collective, the Protectorate. She was hot-headed. A scrapper.

As weight classes went, Regret was in for some rough learning.

He managed to squeeze off two shots at her, both of which hit her cloak and fell useless to the ground. Then she was on him, the fingers of her left hand curled in his armored chest piece like it was nothing. She lifted him off the ground and slapped him unconscious.

Not punched.

Slapped. Open palm. From where I stood, it sounded like the world's largest belly flop, and he was out like a light.

I swear on my father's name, she looked disappointed.

Still holding the limp body of the hitman, she turned to face me. I saw her weighing the costume: rooster mask, brown bodysuit with wide stripes up the side in a deep russet. If she saw the toe spurs, she didn't react. Most heroes didn't wear blades. Too much risk of killing someone, which most heroes were careful about. But I wasn't most heroes.

"Who are you?"

It would have made me happier if she had dropped Regret. The way she held him, feet dangling above the ground like he weighed less than nothing was off-putting. But I suppose it was safer to hold onto him until the police arrived. "They call me Bantam."

"Who calls you that?"

It was a legit question. I worked solo and struck fast, so it wasn't like I had any serious press outside of the fantasy leagues. And I didn't leave business cards. No one had called me much of anything out loud, let alone Bantam. I had been careful. But that had been my father's name when he wore the same costume, and it seemed every person on the damn planet had a camera on their phone now. One more thing to blame Jaccob Stevens and Starcom for, I guess. "People."

It was enough of an answer for her. "Guess that explains the chicken mask." She nodded her head toward the captive. "And what's his name?"

It didn't feel worth it to correct her on the difference between rosters and chickens. "The papers call him Regret."

She laughed, a lighter sound than I would have expected from someone with her presence, her visible strength. The fucker was still hanging there in her grip like a broken doll. "Regret? Oh, that's got to suck for him. Did he lose a bet?"

"You'll have to ask him," I said. "While you're at it, you might want to ask who hired him."

I imagine her eyebrows shot up beneath her mask though I couldn't see it. Her entire demeanor shifted. "He's a contract hitter?"

"Yes. No idea who hired him, but his intended targets are the couple in their fifties currently hiding out in the bar, likely reeking of their own urine and covered in the remains of that planter over there. I'd really like to know why they were targets."

Velvet looked in the direction of the bar, spotted the planter, looked back to Regret, then back to me in quick succession. "And why should I trust you?"

"Because I held your playmate there off long enough for you to get here and stop him," I said. I heard the approach of sirens. This part of town, they were likely from my precinct, too. I couldn't linger. "Roof of St. Joan at midnight. I'll share what I know."

I got half of a nod from her. It was enough. Midnight was still a few hours away. Plenty of time for me to do some digging. I bolted for the stairs and took them two at a time until I hit the rooftop, somewhat winded. I wasn't cut out for this. I knew it. Hell, Velvet probably knew it as well.

But I needed to know. It was going to drive me crazy if I didn't. I took a few seconds on the rooftop to catch my breath before plunging off the north side of the building.

Arms out to my side, the glider fins caught the air, sent me soaring on a thermal updraft. I rode it all the way to my downtown apartment, sighting on the yellow rug hung over the railings as an easy marker.

I opened up the plastic tool box stashed under the folding chair on my tiny patio and rooted through the plastic baggies of incense until I found the pack of cigarettes I had buried there. I only allowed myself one a day, and damn if I hadn't earned it today. Mask on the table next to me, I opened the sliding glass door to let my apartment cool off a bit while I sat at the little bistro table in the dark and smoked.

Violence was a funny thing. In the heat of the moment, anyone could be a target. But premeditated violence was something different. Enough forethought to hire someone to do the killing— that was something ugly and cold. It was impersonal, wanting someone dead but not needing the release of doing the act yourself, in fact cultivating that distance from the target.

In my experience, there were three kinds of people who went that route: someone who didn't want to get caught, someone who wasn't capable of doing the act themselves, or someone who simply believed the other person flat out just needed to die.

It made me wonder which we were dealing with.

And why.

CHAPTER THREE—XIA LO

Xia Lo crouched in the crossbeams, back pressed against the corrugated steel of the warehouse ceiling. She had been there for close to an hour, waiting for the four Kings to gather beneath her roost. Motionless and silent, she was like a shadow within deeper shadow, eternal patience and the certainty of death made manifest. She was confident they would not see her even if they thought to look up. Even if they scanned the darkness with digital probes, the jester-like costume of the Harlequin would screen her presence. It wasn't that she didn't trust the Kings. If she couldn't trust them or, more importantly, if Uncle Donald couldn't trust them, they would be dealt with. But for all intents and purposes, the four Kings, the infamous Crime Kings of Cobalt City, were loyal to the Lo family.

Trusting them to not test boundaries against each other was another matter, however. Gang politics were gang politics, after all.

The concept of the Crime Kings was almost as old as Cobalt City. Just as the idea of heroes took root and flourished the fertile New England soil following the Revolutionary War, so too did the idea of organized master criminals. The makeup of the Kings changed over time. Masters of crime guilds in one era, charismatic megafauna in another. Following a massive war between the Crime Kings in the sixties, Donald Lo had stepped in and restored order that has held for four decades, bringing all four Kings under his house.

It was called "organized crime" for a reason, and under Lo leadership it had not been so well organized since the days of Peppermint Nick in the period between world wars. The various avenues of crime had been broken up and dispersed between four newly organized gangs, each with their own area of specialty. Each

King had a hierarchy—an Ace for enforcement, a Queen for administration, and a Jack as a lieutenant with a gang structured below that answered only to them, just as each of the Kings answered to Donald Lo through an intermediary. That intermediary had been Xia Lo in the guise of the Harlequin for more than a decade now, a task she had been trained for since being sent to live with her Uncle Donald as a child.

Not that she had ever been a child.

Not really.

She rationalized that it was a tradeoff. She had a secure lifestyle and the best toys dirty money could buy, but didn't have as much control over her own life as she'd like. Most of her time was dedicated to running family affairs as the Harlequin, complete with a ballistic weave suit that made her invisible to electronics, a jester face helmet with full sensor array, and a high-tech ceramic staff tricked out with a suite of weaponry that leveled just about any playing field.

The Kings of Crime were big fish in their individual pools, but she was a shark, and they were merely fatty tuna to her.

She heard soft-soled shoes approaching from between the stacks of wooden shipping crates, heralding the arrival of the first King. She knew who it was before he stepped into the light, identified by his fondness for tennis shoes and a slightly irregular gait caused by a bullet that had lodged in his hip two years ago. Blake was blonde with the exaggerated, shirt-straining musculature of a die-hard gym rat. Holding the title of the King of Clubs, he was in charge of extortion and blackmail, with a crew that ran almost eighty people deep last time Xia audited the rolls. He had come up through the ranks and was what her uncle considered a perfect soldier—loyal to a fault and completely lacking in ambition. As long as Blake got to bust the occasional head and had the money and respect he was due, he was a constant. He took his seat at the table below Xia's perch and waited, squeezing the life out of a blue racquet ball with a hand the size of a roasted duck.

He didn't have long to wait before he was joined by Emilio, the King of Diamonds. Emilio was heavy set, bald, in his early fifties. He looked like someone's uncle, easy smile, deceptively good natured. He ran a seventy-person gang specializing in robbery and fencing—a modern day Fagin, if Fagin was an Italian lighting fixture wholesaler. If a person needed something liberated or liquidated, Emilio's crew could do it. He'd been working for the Lo family for over thirty years in some capacity. He had the family's trust, but Xia had never much cared for him. His gaze always lingered on her a little too long. She knew about his fetish for Asian girls. There had been so many indiscretions with the girls at the Forbidden Palace Casino & Hotel that he would have been banned were it not for his connection to the family.

"Blake," he bellowed with mock cheer, "Can I have someone bring you a protein shake or maybe something heavy to lift?"

Blake seemed lost in meditation and didn't rise to the taunt. It looked like Emilio was going to push it when the back door opened to admit another King.

High heels clicked across the concrete as a stately black woman strode through the door, close-cropped Afro peppered with gray and a tailored black suit worn over a simple white shirt with a banded collar. Though Emilio might be a year or so older than Monica, she'd been in charge of her gang for longer, and had a crew that numbered close to two hundred. When Monica took over the gang, it had been called the Spades, but she had changed it to the Swords to reflect the nature of her domain as well as her fondness for tarot cards. She was one of the big money makers for the Lo family, in charge of both drug and weapon smuggling. She maintained control of her domain with an iron fist. The handful of people who had risen up to challenge her had all been dealt with ferociously—memorably. Of all of the Kings of Crime, she was the only one who Xia Lo respected. Monica had paid a blood price to get her crown, and she maintained it with blood.

"Looks like we're waiting for Tomas again," Monica said, taking her customary seat. She leaned forward, took a small notebook out of her breast pocket and put it and a pen to her right before crossing her hands on the table before her to wait.

"Tomas and the Harlequin," Blake said.

Xia couldn't see Monica's smile from where she was, but she could hear it in her voice.

"Oh? I always assume she's everywhere."

Emilio scoffed. He took his seat and leaned back and put his feet up on the table. "That's stupid," he said looking directly at Xia Lo in the deep shadows but not seeing her.

"I view her a bit like God," Monica said. "I figure it's better to act as if she's there at all times and be wrong than to risk assuming she's not there and be wrong. Because none of us are above being smote with biblical precision."

"Big talk for a woman who peddles guns and drugs to her own community," Emilio said.

Like Blake, she was practiced at not rising to Emilio's taunts. It was his tactic. Bait, feint, get them in close, and open their throat. Xia Lo had seen him do it in a fight with a Jack who challenged his crown a few years ago. A hidden straight razor settled that matter and discouraged anyone in his organization from challenging the old man again.

"Yes, but I also peddle to your community, Emilio," she said calmly. "Ain't no one going broke feeding the vices of impotent old white men with too much money. Death is an equal opportunity employer."

Death was also the one thing none of the Kings had domain over. In his unquestionable wisdom, Donald Lo decided that no one gang should be given ownership over death. They could defend themselves all they liked. But organized, premeditated murder had to be sanctioned. That fell to Xia Lo. She would either handle it herself, sub-contract it out to any number of freelance operatives on the Lo family books, or give the petitioning King permission to handle it themselves. Each solution had its own benefits and risks.

The King of Hearts, Tomas, finally showed up twelve minutes late. His lack of respect for their time would be noted in Xia's report to her uncle. "I suppose you have a good excuse for your tardiness," she said from the darkness above the table.

The look on Emilio's face was priceless.

"Had some palms to grease that required the personal touch," Tomas said, his Russian accent as thick as when he arrived in Cobalt City a decade ago. He was lean like a wolf, and in his late thirties, he was the youngest of the Kings. Unlike the others, he was also ambitious. The Lo family had recruited him shortly after his arrival in Cobalt City, positioning him to run the Hearts gang, responsible for prostitution and human trafficking due to his personal experience doing similar work for a Russian cartel in New York. He was a King of Crime now, but both Xia and her uncle knew he had sights set higher than that. He ran a gang of over a hundred deeply unpleasant individuals. His ego made it seem he believed he could run the whole city if given a chance.

Xia dropped to the ground at the edge of the table, the reactive cushioning in her boots absorbing the impact from the thirty-foot drop. "Then I suppose you'll give your report first."

Tomas shrugged, setting into his seat. "Business is good. We have a container coming in later this week with fresh product, most of which already has buyers lined up. I have my brokers looking for placements for the rest. As for recruiting, we're meeting quotas and seeing a return on investment that's fifteen percent above this time last year."

"Fifteen percent?" Monica said, rolling her eyes.

"Tech conference in April," Tomas said with a shrug. "They had needs and the money to have those needs met. Plus, they were from out of town, so they were ready to party like Caligula with no one around judging them. I'm surprised we didn't hit eighteen percent growth."

"Swords?" Xia said.

"We're getting some undue attention on two fronts," Monica said. "Mister Grey from the Protectorate is coming down hard on our operations in Karlsburg. He shut down two distribution centers—one eight days ago, the second five days later. And Gato Loco broke up an arms delivery in Quayside two nights ago. Profits are good, and personnel numbers will rebound from those hits. But we could stand to have some of the heat shifted, and we need an infusion of inventory."

Xia had heard about the arms delivery mess, but was surprised she hadn't heard about the distribution center until now. "Was Mister Grey acting solo or with the Protectorate?"

"Our people say it was solo. He's taking the war on drugs thing rather personally. I've called in a contractor from out of town to deal with him, but a little breathing room would be welcome."

"I'll see what I can do to shift his attentions over to the Pumpkin King up in Morriston and northern Karlsburg. That should buy you some time to shift your distribution centers. As for the inventory, I'll have to see what I can do. Send me a list of what you need."

"Speaking of undue pressures," Blake said, "I can't speak for anyone else, but I've had someone picking around the edges of my operations. I'm losing a bagman here, a leg breaker there. Whoever is doing it is staying below the radar, moving fast and not leaving a trail. My guys don't even know what the bastard looks like. It's starting to be a problem, and I don't have any capes to point to. If it wasn't so precise, I'd almost think it was another gang trying to edge us out."

"I'm with Blondie," Emilio said. "I've had three different B&E crews shut down in the past two weeks. The first couple were two-man crews, but the third one was a full four-man house sweeper team. None of them saw a damn thing. One minute fine, the next minute, pop."

It was rare for Emilio and Blake to agree on something, especially something business related. It didn't bode well. "No witnesses?" Both men shook their heads. "No sign of unusual weapons or superpowers?"

"Just bruising," Blake said. "Oh, and one of the breakers got sliced, but that could have been from the window he was kicked through or something in the alley three floors below that he landed in."

"What neighborhoods?"

Both men answered "Downtown," without hesitation.

Xia nodded her oversized jester-faced mask. She waited for them to volunteer up any additional information, and when they didn't, she turned to the other Kings. "Have either of you had similar problems?"

Monica shifted uncomfortably. "I lost two low-level distributors in downtown, one last week and one the week before. Honestly, I figured it was a rival crew looking for a quick score and doubled up their protection."

"And I had a broker get sent to the hospital three days ago," Tomas offered, "but he had been shot twice, so I doubt it's the same guy."

"I'll take care of it," Harlequin said. "And if it happens again, let me know immediately when and where. And send me the details of the previous attacks when we're done here."

"You know who this is?" Emilio said. There was a note of accusation in his tone that didn't sit well with Xia Lo.

She fixed him with her large black eyes for a full minute until he looked away.

"Now," she continued, "let's get on with the reporting and then I'll give marching orders."

CHAPTER FOUR—VELVET

The view from the top of the Basilica of St. Joan was almost as beautiful as the view from inside. Built over a period of seven years starting in 1921, one year after St. Joan of Arc was canonized, the basilica was one of the very few Art Deco places of worship of that scale in the world. Only the Basilica of the Sacred Heart in Brussels was larger. The copper-plated roof had oxidized in the intervening decades and was now a beautiful shade of green. The two towers on the southern side perfectly framed the glow from Starcom Tower.

It was almost pretty enough to make me wish I was Catholic.

I waited on the roof with what little information I'd gathered. I could only assume that this Bantam would bother showing up because she'd suggested the meeting. Considering how quickly she fled the scene, I figured a no-show was more likely. Still, it was worth a gamble, and midnight was hours before my typical bedtime. Say what you will about the hard partying lifestyle, it prepared me for late nights.

The police arrived to take Regret off my hands only minutes after Bantam vanished. It left me little opportunity to shake information out of the hitman, just the name of his targets and that they deserved to die. As far as the potential victims were concerned, a Louis and Mary Pickford, they had nothing in their record that would typically make them the target of an assassination. The husband had some minor drug arrests but had managed to avoid serious jail time, and they had both been cited for disturbing the peace, but they had no apparent connection to larger organized crime. Both of them lived in neighboring Danvers,

Massachusetts, and were decidedly lower-middle class. Louis was a mechanic and Mary a part-time nurse. They were registered at the Cooke Hotel, which might ordinarily be out of their price range, but for a couple playing tourist, it didn't raise any red flags.

So why had someone wanted them dead?

"I was wondering if you'd show up or not," Bantam said from the shadows of the basilica's southeast tower. "Did our paid killer give up his client?"

"No. And I didn't see anything in the target's history that explained the hit."

Bantam paced the roof, rolling her shoulders as if to loosen them up. I wondered how she had gotten here, if she had climbed the basilica or had some other means of transport. "Regret doesn't work for free, but he's new to Cobalt. He might be working a sliding scale to accommodate clients with less money. He was a mob hitter in New York until he lost his family in the crossfire, and he decided to go freelance. If the targets had organized crime connections, I'd even consider the possibility that he did this one for free."

"Nothing indicates serious crime connections," I said, then impulsively added, "Unlike you."

Bantam froze as if anticipating more, or maybe an attack. When none came, she relaxed slightly, but I could tell she was still ready to bolt if necessary. "Well, that's a fascinating change of conversation."

"A friend told me there used to be a Bantam that worked Cobalt City, enforcer for the Lo syndicate."

"Emphasis on used to be. That Bantam was a guy and he vanished off the scene something like fifteen years ago."

Oh yeah. I probably should have asked Archon how long ago that other Bantam was active. Too bad I had been in a hurry.

"So, no connection?"

"Same tailor. No connections that matter."

Not the most reassuring answer, but she had helped me out earlier. And she'd shown up, which suggested that either she really wanted to know the answers to this case, or she had a few answers of her own. That put her on the side of angels for the time being. If she got squirrely with me, I didn't doubt I could put her down.

"Ok. Fair enough. Did you manage to find anything?"

"Just that unlike you, I'm not so sure about their lack of ties to something big. Did you look into their financials?"

"Just the last few years. Nothing stood out."

Even behind the full full face mask she exuded a cocky confidence. It left me guessing if the woman fancied herself a detective of some sort. "Twelve years ago they received a lump sum payment from a private account of $60,000."

Okay. That raised some flags. The husband worked as a mechanic now, but it was always possible he had done something else for a living twelve years ago. "Were they living in Danvers at the time?"

"Yes—" It was a measured response, as if she was gauging my reaction, seeing if I could catch up. It was condescending, and I didn't much care for it. "The whole family lived there as far back as is relevant."

"Danvers isn't exactly a hotbed of criminal activity," I said. Understatement of the year. It was a town north of Boston, population sitting somewhere around 25,000, and more well-known for the creepy, and now shuttered, state mental hospital than anything else.

"Maybe," Bantam conceded. "Or maybe you're thinking of the wrong kind of crime. Twelve years ago, the Pickfords had a fourteen year old daughter named Astrid. Police took witness statements at the Cooke following the attempted hit. One of the witnesses gave her name as Astrid Perdu."

Perdu. French for lost. What the actual fuck? My stomach tightened the way it always did when I was about to look at something I knew I couldn't un-see. "*Had* a daughter? What happened to her? Because if this is a ghost thing, it's out of my pay grade. I can't punch a ghost."

"Can't punch this either. The story is runaway. Or so they said at the time."

"So she ran away from home and came after them over a decade later? I mean, if it's really her?"

"It's either her or one hell of a coincidence. Now I have 60,000 reasons to think it bears looking into."

I wasn't sure what she was implying, but at least the idea that Astrid was a ghost stalking her parents was likely off the table now. Stranger things had happened in this city. But I was invested now, and I'd hate to hand this off to Mister Grey just because as the

Protectorate's resident undead he was better suited to dealing with ghosts. "You managed to get a look at police statements. Did you get her address?"

Bantam flashed a scrap of paper. The summer wind off Cape Cod whipped it about in her thin fingertips. "I'm new, but I'm not *that* new. It's a Quayside address, a motel a few blocks off Casino Row called the Close-Inn."

I wasn't familiar with it, but knew Casino Row well enough. I popped open a pouch on my belt and pulled out my map. Closed up, it looked like a pair of fat pen-like cylinders side by side. I depressed the top and pulled them apart, unspooling a micron-thin screen from the cylinder on the left, 5" x 7" with our current location shown from a satellite view. "Close-Inn Motel, Quayside." The image scrolled rapidly, putting a red dot over a run-down L-shaped motel across the river.

"Zoom out. Flag landmarks." The view pulled back far enough to show Casino Row, and flagged Wylie's Wild West three blocks south, two blocks east of our destination. Easy. I could sight on the neon waving cowboy sign from a mile away. I put the map away. "Do you have a way to get there?"

Bantam tapped her wrists against her belt and put her arms out to the side to reveal a thin membrane stretched along her side. "Glider wings."

From where we were the north side of Downtown, across the river into Quayside, I would have time to stop for coffee by the time she got there. I didn't want to be insult her. Our working relationship was too new to risk that, but I had to offer other options. "I can get us there in a hop, skip, and a jump if you don't mind being carried."

I could see her considering. She was used to operating solo, dependent on herself for everything. Even now that I'd been part of a team, it was difficult for me to accept help. I totally got it.

"Half of the Protectorate has no movement powers, they're stuck at ground level, so you're already miles ahead of them with the glider wings, trust me," I said. "But if you want to do this fast, hop on my back. It's how I've had to carry Huntsman around."

That seemed to overcome her reluctance. Huntsman was a legacy hero. He'd been around since we were still fighting the Redcoats. Or at least his ancestors had been. If getting a piggyback ride from me was good enough for him, it was good enough for Bantam.

She climbed onto my back, chin nestled on my shoulder, surprisingly strong legs around my waist, ankles locked together securely. "Trust me. I've never lost a passenger yet, but it does take a little getting used to."

Bantam chuckled softly, and I could feel her breath, warm against my cheek. Her breath smelled faintly like cardamom and coffee, which was not the least bit unpleasant. "If I fall, I can glide to safety easily enough. Don't worry about me."

With a smile, I took a few swift steps to the southern edge of the basilica roof and leapt. For all her bravado, I heard Bantam gasp. She knew I could jump, but experiencing it firsthand was another thing entirely. I cleared the glittering beacon of Starcom, below and to the left, with the first bound, landing on the curved, white roof of Bishop Area on the south side of downtown. Another quick set of steps to reorient, and a second leap put me across the river on the roof of a warehouse two blocks from our destination, barely missing the huge orange cranes on the southern banks of the river, feeding the Quayside docks. A final short hop put us in the alley behind the motel, landing hard enough that we triggered two nearby car alarms, both of which I immediately switched off with a kill-trigger in my belt pouch.

Bantam disengaged calmly. "Thanks. That was much quicker."

"Anytime." *Wait. Am I blushing? That's unexpected. Damn it, Julianna ... good thing it's too dark back here for anyone to notice.*

It had cooled off to a balmy but still muggy seventy degrees, almost nice enough I didn't mind the extra weight of the cloak. At least the trip over the river had been refreshing. The smell of water from where the river met Cape Cod just to the east was mixed with the smell of diesel from the warehousing and shipyards between us and the banks. The Close-Inn was two floors of faded paint and regret, its parking lot half-full with Massachusetts plates, only a few from out of state. Buzzing green and red neon tubes framed a signboard that advertised "Cable TV – Weekly – Nightly – Hourly."

"Classy place," I muttered.

Bantam started for the stairs to the second floor walkway. "I pity the poor tourists who were looking for a bargain and got stuck here overnight."

"What room?"

"214. The light is off. Should we knock or give it a try?"

I hadn't even considered *not* knocking. "What do you mean by 'give it a try'?"

"I mean, do we wake her up by knocking or do we wake her up standing over her bed in the dark?"

"Knock!" I said perhaps a bit too loudly. Standing over her bed in the dark? Who *does* that? Bantam shrugged like it was nothing. It made me wonder where she was on that spectrum of hero to vigilante. I mean, it's one thing to be a bad girl. That has mystique and everything. But when you were almost as bad as the criminals you were stopping, it's time for an intervention.

Bantam went to the door and rapped lightly twice. She waited for the lights to come on inside, for some sound of movement, any sign that someone was home. Nothing. She rapped again, this time hard enough that it might have woken up the people in the adjoining rooms if anyone was trying to sleep there. No lights went on anywhere. No sound. She looked over her shoulder at me as if asking for permission.

I nodded, and she set to picking the lock with speed and precision. We were inside within seconds, but Bantam froze up three steps inside the door.

"Don't touch anything."

It took a moment for my eyes to adjust to the darkness of the room, but once it did, I saw what made her hesitate. Nothing like a corpse to add a layer of mystery to the evening. It was Astrid, sure as shit. I recognized her from the crowd gathered at the Cooke Hotel. She was sprawled out on the green and red patterned comforter in a pool of vomit, long hair fanned out behind her like a golden wing. I knew an overdose when I saw it, and the empty pill and booze bottles on the nightstand screamed an intentional checking out. A battered manila envelope stuck up between two square whiskey bottles like a paper tombstone.

She was dressed in jeans and t-shirt with trashy red pumps kicked off at the foot of the bed. In the half-light from the parking lot, it looked like she was renting this place by the week. It had an orderly, lived-in look. I checked the chipped dresser drawers to see clothes carefully folded within the top one, what I could only describe as fetish-wear in the bottom drawer, along with an assortment of sex toys.

"If this is the daughter, she doesn't have anything to tell us," I said.

I looked over my shoulder to see Bantam looking the manila envelope from the nightstand, mini-flashlight pinched between the fingers of one hand. "No, she told us plenty."

"What did you find?"

"Motive? Suicide note? Saddest Lifetime movie plot ever? Call it whatever you want." She dropped the scraps of paper back into the envelope and tossed it to the end of the bed near me.

I picked it up to flip through, but Bantam took the liberty of summarizing as I scanned the pictures, photo-copied documents, and hand-written pages. "Her parents sold her when she was fourteen to a man named Samuel White in Boston. He kept Astrid for four years, probably until she aged out of whatever his particular desired age range was. Then he essentially sold her to a pimp in Boston who ran her until she managed to break away three years later. She hit Cobalt City somewhere around age twenty-one, tried to go straight but kept falling into patterns. Worked as a dancer in a few clubs in The Hollows, tricks on the side to build up a bankroll, couldn't break the cycle, couldn't get clean, and couldn't live with it anymore. Lured her parents to Cobalt City with a letter, asking for reconciliation. There's a photocopy in the file for convenience. Then she used what was left of her bankroll to hire Regret to kill them."

My hands were trembling as I turned the pages. The document trail backed up everything Bantam was telling me. Photos of Astrid with her parents told a complicated picture. Some were the typical sullen family photos of an unhappy child, her frowning over a birthday cake or arms crossed in defiance at a family picnic. And there were some that I wished I'd never seen: seductive poses from a scantily clad girl who looked to be no more than ten, pictures of her dressed up like a princess at Halloween, images of innocence that never touched her eyes. Those eyes had seen too much.

We had stopped her vengeance. I looked at her body on the narrow bed and wondered if she'd still be alive if we'd failed, if she had only died because she couldn't live in a world with her parents anymore. Had her suicide been a release from whatever life she'd been living, or an attempt to avoid consequences of having hired a hitman?

"Make sure to leave the file where the police will find it," Bantam said, pocketing her tiny flashlight.

My stomach was clenching up again. I needed to throw up, but didn't want to do it here. It took everything I had to choke the bile back. I had seen her parents. I had seen the monsters who had done this to her, who had groomed their own daughter to feed the sexual desires of other monsters.

They had looked like normal people. Boring. If I had sat next to them on an airplane, I would have forgotten them by the time I stepped into the concourse.

"It's a lot to process," Bantam said.

I didn't understand how she could be so calm. I wanted to punch something. Anything. My free hand kept clenching and unclenching. If I had been holding a steel pipe, I might have twisted it into a pretzel without even noticing. "It's too much to process."

I hunched down, tried some deep breathing to get my nausea under control.

"We should probably get out of here soon, call this in to the police."

"Why doesn't this bother you?" I snapped. I know I snapped. There would be time to feel horrible about it afterward, but fuck, it was way too late, and I wasn't up to being polite at the moment.

Bantam stared daggers at me. No mask could hide the anger. "Excuse me?"

"Why aren't you freaking out?"

"Because freaking out doesn't solve anything," she said calmly. "But don't think this doesn't bother me. It does. It always has. It probably always will."

It hit me like a slap. "What?"

"You think this is unique? You think this is a new story? Princess, you have no idea."

I shot to my feet and was across the room in a blink. To her credit, Bantam barely flinched though I could have smacked her through the seedy motel room window had I chosen to. The way my fist was clenched, I'm not proud to realize that impulse was closer than I would have liked. "Who are you calling Princess?"

"You," Bantam said.

Jesus, but she has guts. I'll give her that.

30

"You're Sleeping fucking Beauty," she continued. "But instead of a kiss, something else woke you up, and you're realizing that this entire time you've been asleep, and the world is rotting from the inside out. I'm happy you're awake and everything, but some of us have been slogging through this shit for a while."

I backed down. She wasn't the bad guy here. I knew that. I *knew* that. And just because I wanted to hit someone didn't mean there was anyone to hit. Not here, at least. Not now.

"I didn't think this kind of thing happened here."

Bantam sighed. Her shoulders slumped. "I know. I'm sorry. This is a rude damn awakening. If you need some time, I understand. I can find my way home and deal with contacting the police."

"No."

She paused, taken aback. "What?"

"No. I don't need some time. I need to—" *hit* "—do something."

It was like she was actually seeing me for the first time. "You're serious?"

"As a barium enema."

She chuckled despite herself. "You have no idea what you're getting into."

"I know," I said. I didn't know her. I didn't really know if I could trust her. But I had also been around the hero game long enough to sense when I was in over my head. I knew when I needed to ask for help. And she was as close to a local guide as I was likely to get. Archon may be smart, but even I knew there was a difference between knowing facts and understanding something. "Are you willing to show me?"

She smiled in a way that I'm quite sure made me blush again.

"Do you like doughnuts?"

I was sidelined by the question for a few seconds. "Um ... who doesn't?"

"Communists. Okay, put the envelope back the nightstand. Let's close this up. What I'm going to tell you is going to require two crullers, minimum."

"You're serious?" I returned the ticking time-bomb to the nightstand and followed her out to the walkway.

"I never kid about doughnuts. And I know just the place."

31

CHAPTER FIVE—BANTAM

I don't know how Velvet has been in the hero game as long as she's claimed yet never heard of Super Doughnut. Built in the fifties, it was a block off the intersection between Mid-Cape Highway and Casino Row, a sweeping wing of bold red steel above a glass-enclosed circle of light that promised frosted fried dough 24-7. Not only did they have the best crullers in town, they also catered to the superhero crowd, whether by design or quirk. There was even a covered picnic table on the roof with no stair or ladder access. If you couldn't fly, jump, or climb like a tree-frog, you were piss outta luck.

If I wasn't able to glide over from the billboard on the edge of the parking lot, I'd have fallen in with the piss outta luck crowd. But I'll make that extra effort for somewhere to enjoy a doughnut. Aram, the skinny Armenian kid who usually worked the register, knew my order by heart. I added two chocolate-chocolate with peanut to my usual order, along with two cans of Boss Black, a canned coffee from Japan that had become something of an acquired taste despite the intense bitterness.

"Team-up tonight?" Aram said with an eager smile. When you're single, people always want to set you up with their friends. When you're a solo hero, they always push for a team-up. I think Aram was concerned that I was becoming the superhero equivalent of a cat lady. I didn't share his concern, but didn't think he was wrong, either. I liked my independence.

Velvet was waiting for me on the rooftop when I arrived with the greasy white paper bag. "I could have gotten that," she said.

"My invite, my treat. It's only doughnuts, anyway. We go somewhere fancy, we can see if you carry cash in your utility belt. Or maybe the Protectorate gives you a gold card or something."

I sat at the table and removed my mask. It was a calculated risk. The table was screened, so I wasn't worried about someone outside figuring out my identity. And I figured if Velvet really wanted to figure out who I was beneath the mask, she had the resources of the Protectorate to do so. Removing the mask was a sign of trust. It transformed me from a woman wearing a superhero costume with a bit of historical baggage to a Korean woman in her thirties with fairly un-remarkable features and an appreciation for a good doughnut.

The fact that Velvet didn't remove her mask told me a few things. One, the obvious fact that her domino-style mask didn't have to be removed to allow her to eat. Two, she didn't trust me yet. Three, there was a good chance I'd recognize her, which implied she was at least a minor celebrity around town in her regular life. I filed this away for future reference.

"Watch out for the coffee," I said passing the can over to her. "It has a hell of a bite."

She popped the tab and took a sip with a wince. "Damn. And I thought I was bitter!"

I smiled reluctantly. We were both avoiding why we were here, both needing a bit of sugar and dough to soften the blow of the coming conversation. I let us both get one doughnut in before I started.

"Ok, so what you saw tonight ... it isn't as uncommon as anyone would like," I said carefully. "But it's easier for people to just pretend it isn't happening and look the other way than actually confront. I don't know how it got that way. I don't know how we let ourselves get here, but that's where we are now. It's not just other countries. It's not just Thailand or Eastern Europe, or a bunch of kinky Sheiks in Saudi Arabia, and thinking that it is allows people to distance themselves. It lets them think it's *them* and not *us* so they don't have to deal with it. Human trafficking, sex-slavery? It makes more money than big fast food chains here in the U.S. alone. I'm talking billions of dollars."

I watched her face go through stages of disbelief and denial beneath that midnight blue oval of mask around her eyes. I gave her time to process it before hitting her with the other fist.

34

"And the biggest problem is, it's not centralized."

Her brow furrowed slightly. "Hold up. What do you mean?"

"Think of unregistered assault weapons or cocaine as a comparison," I tried. "Whether you want a single gun or a baggie of coke, that supply chain can usually be traced back to a handful of sources that deal in bulk and feed it out through subordinates. Sure, you might find a guy who is selling something he came into possession of through other means, but it's rare. Real rare. It's far more common to have established channels of distributions."

I watched her sip on the bitter canned coffee while she processed.

"So," she said, "what about large scale trafficking? Are there, I don't know, slavery rings that do this on a bigger scale? I remember my dad telling me stories to keep me in line when I was younger. Typical dad horror stories of pretty American girls getting drugged and sold overseas."

"It happens," I admitted. "Sometimes sold overseas. Sometimes sold domestically. And there are organizations that bring people over here with promises of husbands or work and then sell them to the higher bidder. Some go to brothels, some to video sex chat lines, some to private buyers, but most of them get sold into mundane commercial services: house cleaning, food service, etc. It's a gray area."

I could tell I was losing her. Some things are easy to accept in the abstract but the more that gets revealed the more unbelievable it gets. This rabbit hole went deep and it went wide. I knew. I'd taken that trip years ago. Once you started digging, started seeing the rot in the system that others just glossed over, you started to question everything. It was a lot to swallow, that things were so broken that people would rather just look the other way. I let her fumble around in the dark for a bit then gave her some specifics to help ground her—to help make things more concrete.

"There is a major candy company in Pennsylvania," I said slowly, making sure she was really listening. "They offered a sort of work-study program for foreign students. Come to America, work for them, they'll provide housing and you get a chance to play tourist. Sweet deal, right?"

"It was a scam? It was some other front?"

I shook my head. "No, it was the right company. And the program did give these kids jobs and a place to stay. But it was like the classic sharecropper trap. The company didn't pay as much as they said they would, and deducted housing costs from the checks to put them in these sub-standard worker dorms. Sure, they had the chance to play tourist, but they were in a factory town with nothing to see, and no money go get out. Stuck. Word got out and the hammer came down on them. It made national news for a day or two, but page six news. And it was forgotten about within weeks. I mean, this is the same industry that openly uses child slaves to harvest cocoa in western Africa and it doesn't stop people from buying their cheap chocolate bars to give away to kids every Halloween. There's irony for you."

"But the program stateside got shut down while they did nothing to the one in Africa?"

I shrugged. "The one in Pennsylvania got shuttered for a while. I don't know if it started again in a slightly revised form with a new group of students. It had been going on for a long time. I don't even know if that was the first time it got discovered and rebuked. I'm not one of these people to shout that Capitalism is evil, but the purpose of business is to make money. An organization gets big enough, you're going to end up with a percentage of people in charge who don't give a shit on how they save money as long as doesn't come out of their paychecks."

Velvet chewed on her doughnut. We listened to late-night truckers pull past on their way to the riverside docks, to people below us picking up a few apple fritters on the way home from the bars. "Ok, so, that sort of touches on large scale distribution," she said, proving she'd been paying attention. "But that doesn't explain Astrid."

I nodded and tried to figure out how to start. "Ok, so there are some real fucking monsters out there. Not the kinds who wear masks and try to crush banks, but people who don't give a damn about anything but themselves. People with zero conscience, zero compassion. People who go to their jobs and live their lives and don't care whose life they might ruin. Sometimes, those people have kids. Whether it's their own kids or they get involved with someone who is just at the end of their rope with their own kids. Kids in the foster system, who get bounced from house to house to house—they're particularly vulnerable, which I hate saying, because there are really great foster parents out there. But there are really bad ones, too."

"But I don't see the jump from being an abuser to a ... what ... seller? Slaver?"

"Not all of these people are abusers. Not really. The common denominator is that a lot of them just see the kids as property, as a factor in a financial equation of sorts. But the people who do have a taste for kids, the predators, they learn to hide what they are from most people. They talk in code to find their own kind, or to find people who are ... receptive. They hear some guy at work talking about their kid with a certain amount of disdain, they might perk up a little bit. They might go over for a few beers and the basketball game some day and get ideas. Pretty soon, the parent, the person who is supposed to take care of and protect these children, sees the predator as a source of income. And before you know it, they're pocketing cash to let their five year old sit on 'Uncle Jerry's' knee for a bit."

"This sounds an awful lot like conspiracy theories," Velvet said, grasping for any exit out of the moral quicksand she had slipped into. "Conspiracy theories or urban legends."

"Was Astrid an urban legend?"

She closed off, leaned back from me a bit. "That's not fair. She's one person. A data point, not a trend."

I had hoped for more. For better. For her to maybe stick with it now that eyes were open and not shy away from uncomfortable truths. She was Velvet, the powerhouse princess, strongest woman I'd ever seen in Cobalt City.

I hadn't expected weakness. Not from her. But I didn't know what else to call it.

Fuck, but it was disappointing.

"Give me something," she said into the uncomfortable silence.

"What? Charts? Maybe a heartfelt commercial with a movie star in it? The information is out there if you look. There are around 100,000 kids who find their way into sexual slavery every year. You probably see them and don't even realize what you're seeing."

"I don't want to be a bitch here," she said, which was doubtful at this point. That phrase always tended to precede a bitchy statement. "But this is a lot to believe."

I concentrated on my breathing, good air in, bad air out, clearing toxins and negative emotions with each exhale. My eyes were open but I wasn't seeing her anymore. I was looking inward, at a quiet, internal space. "You're right," I admitted. "It's a lot.

Especially all at once. And it's my fault for diving into some of the harder to accept instances like what we saw tonight. Let's scroll back a bit. I mentioned the two extremes ... the cartels who import people and the ones who sell kids under their protection. They're both real. They're both problems. But I'd hesitate to say they're the most common."

"Let me guess," she said, a wry smile on the corner of her lips where a chocolate doughnut crumb held on tenaciously. "The cliché guy at the bus stop."

"Or train station. Or airport. Or youth hostel," I said. "Cliché, but true. There's a mix of entrepreneuring dickbags and organized gangs built around the practice of finding wide-eyed lost kids fresh into town not knowing where they're going to sleep or where their next meal is coming from. A lot of these kids are runaways, leaving behind horrible situations back home, thinking it can't be any worse out on the street. They're hungry for someone to tell them they're beautiful. That they're loved. And they're being offered somewhere warm to stay. Food to eat. All they have to do is pay their benefactors back."

"And that works?"

I remembered a pimp, a recruiter for the Hearts gang who my department had arrested last year. He was still a kid himself, just turned eighteen. Too bad for him, but lucky for us, because it meant harsher sentencing. He got a whole two years, though he was let go after six months. In his statement, he told officers that the kids in his care had been raped at home so many times, all he had to do was convince them that they should make some money from it.

"Yeah," I said quietly. "It works. A lot of those kids are pretty well broken by the time they step off the bus. There are several independents, but the Hearts gang runs most of the chicken-hawks in Cobalt City. They distribute them to handlers needing to fill their roster. And if they find someone that fits a certain type, someone that they can straight up sell instead of rent, they turn them over to the Concierge."

"Concierge? Like at a hotel? That's ... all kinds of messed up."

"Neutral words make it easier for people to swallow, easier to pretend what they do isn't horrible. Most people who would recoil at the word 'pimp' wouldn't bat an eye at 'handler' or 'party booker' or 'concierge,' but don't let the names fool you."

38

"Do you know who the Concierge is? Or how to find him?"

"No," I lied. Ok, lied slightly. I knew if I upset enough apple carts I could find out who the Concierge was. But that wasn't for me to do. He was a big brick, and I was only chipping away at mortar for now. "He keeps his name out of the papers and his finger on the pulse of the market. He knows who is looking for what. If Astrid's parents didn't broker her sale themselves, then they did it through someone like the Concierge. But twelve years ago, it was almost certainly a different person. There can be a lot of turnover in that kind of racket."

I watched her working through what I'd told her. It seemed like she'd found her courage again, and with it a bit of madness. This was a big, shapeless problem that couldn't be solved by one person swinging at shadows. This wasn't a problem she could punch, but that didn't mean she wouldn't go looking for something to satisfy that impulse. I understood. People like us, we needed to feel like we're making a difference, somehow.

I wondered if I should stop her, maybe deflect her fire toward something more constructive. I had a plan. I'd been working on it for some time, and it was delicate with lots of moving parts. If she went charging in like a drunken cannonball, it could disrupt things. But it might open up other exploits as well. And damn if I wasn't good at thinking on my feet.

"I should be getting back," I said, getting to my feet. "I've got a way home from here, so no need for another lift."

She looked slightly disappointed, which surprised me. "Are you sure? It's no problem."

"And risk you finding my top secret lair? No, I'm good."

She laughed, giving up. It dislodged the doughnut crumb, absolving me of my responsibility to tell her about it. "Well, thanks for the doughnuts and your perspective."

"One last bit of perspective," I offered, "before I go back to my quiet little corner of the city—your biggest enemies in this aren't the Concierge or the Hearts gang or the bad foster parents or trafficking cartels. Your biggest enemies are the people who suspect something is wrong and look the other way because it's too difficult to think about. The indifference and apathy of the masses, that's the dragon that needs slaying."

I left her to chew that over as I sprinted to the end of the angled steel roof and vaulted off into the neon night. My glider wings caught the updraft off the river and I climbed high enough to get to the cargo cranes at a decent elevation. I clambered quickly to the top, sprinted up and out on the extended crane arm, launching myself again. This gave me enough loft to get me within a few blocks of my apartment, up on the roof of a newly remodeled mixed-use building with a sports bar on the ground floor.

I was getting ready to launch off for the final leg of my trip when I heard voices from the street below.

"Who do you think you are, changing your mind?" some random guy shouted from six floors below.

I stepped to the edge and saw a couple below me. The woman was in a short red dress trying to pull away from a man's grip as he led her to a waiting cab. She was trying to talk her way free, but even from here I could tell she was slurring her words. Either she'd had a lot to drink or he'd drugged her. Either was a bad scene. Whatever she'd agreed to with this guy earlier, she definitely wasn't feeling it now.

"You're not even that pretty," he said, not helping his case any. Three people left the bar not fifteen feet from the struggle and said nothing, though the woman in the trio at least slowed down, turned her attention that way. But she didn't stop. The cab driver sat there, engine running, door open, eager to make fare. No one cared that this woman was about to be forced into a vehicle and taken somewhere against her will.

My jaw hurt, and I realized I had been clenching it. Tears stung the corners of my eyes and I realized that I wasn't doing anything to stop it, either.

"No," I whispered. "Fuck that."

I dropped from the rooftop like a shrike. I popped my glider wings to the side with a snap to stop my fall just a few feet from the ground. The woman in the red dress let out a yelp and would have fallen on her ass had loverboy's grip on her forearm not been so fierce. He was surprised, but held his cool relatively well.

"This doesn't concern you," he said, puffing out his chest. I mean, I get it. I'm not a known hero. I don't have a big, scary reputation. I was just a little Korean woman in a rooster mask. And at just over six feet, this guy had almost half a foot and maybe sixty pounds on me. He also had an Ed Hardy shirt with the collar popped, which showed he was prone to bad decisions.

40

"She said no," I said, evenly.

"She's drunk," he said, like that was going to help his case. "She doesn't know what she wants. I'm just taking her home."

"Do you know him?" I asked the woman.

She hesitated, shook her head slightly. "Kind of."

"I'm telling you," he shouted, jabbing a finger at me, "This is none of your goddamned business!"

I grabbed the finger and bent it back in one smooth motion until it touched the back of his hand. He fell to his knees howling and let go of the woman in the process. A double victory as far as I was concerned. Other than the broken finger, which I refused to relinquish yet, I ignored him and kept my attention to the woman. "Do you want to go with him?"

Her "No," was barely above a frightened whisper. I don't know if she was afraid of me or what was going on but I didn't goddamned care.

"You have money for a cab?"

She nodded, and I motioned her toward the waiting cab. The driver had gotten out of his seat and was staring across the roof at me as if wondering if he should engage.

"You get her home safe," I said. "I have your cab number. She gets home safe or what I'll do to you will make what I'm about to do to this fucktrumpet look like a children's birthday party. Understand?"

He nodded and a minute later they were speeding away up Madison.

I turned my attention back to loverboy, who was crying hard enough that snot was bubbling in his left nostril. It was not what one would call a sexy look. "I'm going to make something abundantly clear," I told him in slow, even tones that always seemed to unnerve people who were used to being in control. "No is not a yes. Maybe is not a yes. Drunk and uncertain is not a yes. Passed out is certainly not a yes. The only thing that's a yes is a clear, consensual—no, *enthusiastic*—yes. From now until the grave. Have I made myself perfectly clear?"

He nodded so hard I thought his stupid fucking head was going to snap off and roll into the gutter.

I patted him down in efficient police style for his wallet and checked his driver's license. Blaine. Of course it was a Blaine. I memorized his name and address. "Here's how it's going to be,

41

Blaine. Your date got off unscathed, so I'm going to call it even. But I know who you are. I've got your name and I never forget a face. And I hear everything. You obey the rules I just explained to you, you'll never see me again. You break them, and you'll wish I killed you tonight."

He nodded again.

Heaven help me, I think I might have gotten through to him. If only I could do the same to the thousand other Blaines in Cobalt City.

I was feeling generous and let him go with the broken finger and made my way the final few blocks for a long bath and a few hours of bed.

Never let it be said that I'm not understanding.

CHAPTER SIX—XIA LO

Uncle liked his briefings early, usually over a light breakfast of toast and a medicinal tea he'd been drinking for the past several decades to extend his life. At least he claimed it was the tea that accounted for his longevity. Xia sometimes wondered if he had a painting of himself squirreled away in the sprawling casino he never left, some life-sized portrait depicting him bent and twisted, a grotesquery that reflected his true age and his sins.

Donald Lo hadn't seemed to have aged in the more than thirty years since he had brought her to Cobalt City from The Factory at the tender age of eight. She'd seen pictures of him taken over sixty years ago where the only discernable difference was the width of his lapels.

Uncle Donald sat across the small teak table from her, one hand on the tiny porcelain cup, the other calmly in his lap. "You had the meeting last night?"

Xia was dressed in her normal clothing, a knee length floral skirt, a simple, lacy black blouse over a black camisole. Unlike Uncle, she did not eat at these meetings, no matter how hungry she was. This morning, she was particularly hungry, as work had kept her from a full breakfast earlier. She consoled herself with the thought of the crab Benedict from the hotel kitchen and a pot of black coffee when she was done here.

"I had the meeting last night," she said patiently, knowing full well he was aware she had the meeting. The old man loved his formalities. Loved making people jump through his hoops. "All four of the Kings were present. We need to replace a weapons shipment that Gato Loco broke up. The King of Swords is having her Queen send over a list of what she needs. And we lost a few distribution centers in Karlsburg to the Protectorate."

"There were other, minor losses, as well," he said, proving that he didn't actually need her to give reports. Just one more formality. One more test of loyalty. They would never end, and though she had gotten used to them, she doubted she would ever enjoy them.

Uncle Donald Lo had been the closest thing she had to a father for most of her life. But he had never been ... warm.

"The smaller losses are being dealt with."

He raised a perfectly maintained eyebrow over an ageless brown eye, but said nothing. He set down his tea, picked up a triangle of dry, white toast, and nibbled on a corner of it delicately, like a mouse.

"It's likely that the smaller losses are due to our newest asset."

"An asset who causes losses is not an asset," he said, cold steel in his tone.

She bowed, ceding the point.

"I believe corrections can be made. I believe the losses are small enough to warrant a further investment of patience. We've lost several freelance operatives in recent years—"

"Have we?"

Of course they had. And of course it was open knowledge between them. Xia knew bringing it up risked angering the old man. But for every freelancer lost, more and more responsibilities fell to her. She was capable. No one could question her usefulness. But she was just one person, and she was not without her limits. In the past two years alone, they had lost two assassins, three trusted bagmen, five middle-managers, and an entire R&D team. While she wasn't one-hundred percent certain about the loyalties of their newest asset, especially in wake of recent developments, she felt they could be groomed to replace anyone except the R&D team.

Uncle ate his toast in loaded silence, his attention turned angrily to the task at hand, ignoring Xia for the moment. She told herself she could weather this, just like she weathered everything else. She had earned a degree of personal freedom from him over the years. While she was still bound to him, still subject to his every whim, she still had the freedom to pursue outside interests when time permitted.

Not that time permitted much these days.

She hadn't touched her watercolors in almost a month, a thought that stung like a dagger. Every time she returned to her suite of rooms, the easel and paints set up near the balcony waited for her, dust building up on the blank canvas like snow in winter.

Her uncle washed down the last of the toast with a sip of earthy tea. "When the inventory request comes in from the King of Swords, give her anything she needs. I've forewarned Grant Hamilton. No time to secure another foreign shipment. We'll fulfill with domestic as best as able and eat the cost. Rotate a few pieces of real estate out of the market, let's say five, and consolidate distribution centers to there for now until we have a better, more fortified location. Pumpkin King is looking to expand south. Give him enough rope to hang himself. Draw him out then make him visible. Let our enemies destroy each other while we rebuild some strength."

"And our asset?"

He pursed his lips and looked out the window to his private garden for a long while. The summer breeze billowed the gauzy white curtains as if he'd planned it that way.

"We need to correct disruptive behavior quickly," he said eventually. "Decisively. If it continues to be a problem, or perish the thought, escalates, we'll have to consider harsher measures."

"Yes, Uncle," she said, bowing again.

"Has she benefitted us in any way yet? Is she, in fact, an asset, or just a thorn you are reluctant to remove?"

Xia kept her head down, her gaze on the lacquer finish on the teak table before her. "She has proven useful. Her position grants us easier access to police information that has allowed us to undermine enemy organizations. And we've fed her information that lets the police do our work for us against the Crimean syndicate and the Boston families trying to establish toeholds."

"Successful enterprises?" he asked, his voice slow and cautious.

"Successful campaigns without risking our own resources," Xia said. "All handled quietly without implicating the Lo family. So, yes. Bantam has been a good asset, despite recent indiscretions."

"Her father was of great use to the family at one point," Uncle Donald said, saying nothing he hadn't said a dozen times before. After all, it had been his idea to blackmail Roberta Pak instead of killing her outright, which had been Xia's first instinct. She found it strange that over the past several months, the support had shifted so that she was often the one defending Bantam to her uncle.

"The daughter will be of great use to us as well," Xia said. "Perhaps in ways we can't quite see yet."

Her uncle cracked her across the cheek with the back of his knuckles in a slap that struck like lightning. Xia's temper flared, but she did not move to react.

"Do not presume to lecture me on strategy!"

She felt the red mark her uncle left flare red and angry on her cheek. "I'm sorry, Uncle. That was not my intent."

"Intent is worthless," he said, standing over her, arm cocked to discipline her again should it be necessary. "Action is what matters. I do not care about unforeseen value. I only care about how she can be used, how we can predict her usefulness. What can't be controlled is of no use to us."

Xia remained motionless, let him vent, let him ramble. His body had held up over the long years. But his mind ...

Uncle Donald was not a kind man. And when the cracks showed, he slipped into moments of paranoia, convinced that people were conspiring against him. Fearing that control of the Lo family was slipping, he reacted irrationally. Violently. Not all the losses of Lo family personnel had been the work of heroes or police.

Not two months ago he had tortured one of his trusted bagmen to death, afraid that this loyal employee of fifteen years had been skimming money to start his own operation. It turned out to have been an accounting error, not that the accountant responsible was appropriately reprimanded. Not that would have made any difference to the bagman, lungs filled with wet concrete and dumped in the river.

"My most sincere apologies, Uncle," she said. She felt him pacing behind her, imagined him clenching and unclenching his hand, weighing if he should strike again or not. If she should choose to fight back, she knew she was by far the superior fighter. But that did not matter to Donald Lo. He knew he could hit her with impunity. He always had. She belonged to him. It was his right.

"Do not forget your place," he said through his teeth. "Do not forget how much you owe me."

"I would be nothing without your generosity, Uncle," she said, eyes open.

He paused in his pacing. Then, seemingly satisfied, he grunted and stepped back. "Good. Do as I asked you. There are too many variables in play right now. We must control the ones we can, shut down the others."

Xia Lo unfolded to a standing position and turned to face her uncle. "As you wish. May I go?"

He grunted again, flicked the hand that had struck her in the direction of the door. His mind was already on other things, envisioning the invisible chess board of enemies and allies that only he could see.

She quickly made herself scarce.

The Forbidden Palace Casino & Hotel featured one tower full of rooms, twenty-seven stories high with a pair of penthouse rooms on the top floor, but that was all for the tourists. The real action happened in the main casino building, with gaming, drinking, and concert space on the sprawling ground floor, administrative and security on the second, and private quarters on the third. Uncle Donald alone occupied the fourth floor, comforted by a private Chinese style garden complete with winged gates, cherry trees, and reflecting pools with a slight, arched bridge across the water. She crossed through the garden, feet crunching lightly on the white gravel path to the circular door that led to the elevator foyer.

She wished for another chance to set up her watercolors in the garden. Maybe when the cherry trees were flowering again next year.

Instead, she lingered only briefly at the top of the bridge, looking down into the still waters. She was too used to seeing the white porcelain mask of Harlequin gazing coldly back at her. She could barely recognize the face that looked up from the water now. Emotionless. A killer's face.

She returned to her rooms and considered the work ahead of her today. The watercolors taunted her from the corner near the balcony. She considered packing them up, putting paint and easel and canvas back in the closet. But the thought made her too sad.

"Maybe tomorrow," she said to no one.

CHAPTER SEVEN—VELVET

"So, this other Bantam, he was something of a bad apple, wasn't he?" I said more to myself than to the teammate who had the misfortune of trying to update field reports at the same time as I was doing research.

Archon looked up from the monitor at the other end of the long table in the archives room. "That's one way to put it," he said.

"I mean, he didn't really have superpowers, but he had quite the reputation," I said by way of explanation. I knew I wasn't making sense. I had kind of hit a wall and it was adding to my frustrations.

"Huntsman doesn't have powers," Archon said, "In fact, none of the twenty or so people to wear the mantle of Huntsman had powers. Neither does Gato Loco, to my understanding. Or me, for that matter."

"Or Stardust," I continued his line of thinking. "He just has a genius level intellect and a flying suit of armor complete with energy blasts and more money than the Pope."

"Money is a superpower," Archon said with a wry smile. I'd never stop finding it funny how he could look so statistically average, but be so exceptional in all other regards. He maintained that being statistically average in appearance was in its own way exceptional, in that people tended to forget what he looked like.

"And you're considered the world's foremost expert in pretty much anything," I said. "That's a superpower."

"That's peak conditioning," he said, "but within human parameters. May I ask why you're researching Bantam? He hasn't been seen in ages."

"I spent some time last night with the new Bantam," I said, provoking a perfect, raised eyebrow of incredulity.

"I've heard rumors there's a new one, but I assumed they were a delusion. What is he like?"

"He is a she," I said. I was reminded of the feel of her legs locked around my hips, and the smell of cardamom and coffee on her breath. I hurried on so as not to linger overlong in the memory. "She's more of a hero than the previous Bantam as near as I can tell, just not sure how much more, if you know what I mean. She helped me follow up on that hitman incident yesterday. But she is a bit ... dark."

"So, maybe more of an anti-hero or vigilante rather than a criminal? Interesting choice of legacy to follow, then. I wonder why?"

"I suspect there's some sort of relation. She got the costume from somewhere, whether it was handed down from family or some other connection I don't know. The original Bantam was Asian?"

"No one ever learned his real identity. But yes. Probably Chinese, since he was associated with the Lo family, but they're pretty much equal opportunity. He could have just as easily been Korean or Vietnamese. My guess would be Indonesian based on video I've seen of his fighting style."

"But not Japanese?"

"Not Japanese," Archon said with authority. "The Lo family still holds a deeply personal grudge from the second World War. I don't think we'll ever know the details on that. I'm not sure I want to."

"What happened to the original Bantam? Did he retire or die or just ... vanish?"

"It's a rough life working for organized crime. I sincerely doubt that he retired. That's not the kind of thing a person retires from easily. He was an enforcer. A trained killer. He'd done a lot of dirty work for them over time, and they couldn't just let him go. If he retired, he must have crafted one hell of an escape plan."

"So ... dead?"

"Most likely."

I sucked on my teeth, looking over the available information, including multiple grainy photos of the original Bantam in action.

If what I saw last night wasn't the same suit, it was one hell of an accurate replica.

"So, what kind of follow up did you have with the hitman?" Archon asked, already back to typing in his report.

"We found the person who hired him."

"And turned them over to authorities?"

I shook my head, already looking for an exit to this conversation. "She was already dead."

The staccato clatter of his typing ground to a halt. "Oh."

"Suicide."

"That's one way to avoid prosecution, I suppose. Still tragic."

"Yeah," I said. I didn't want to get into it and bring everything back to the surface. As tragic as suicide was, it was the cream cheese frosting of a truly fucking tragic life. I didn't want to explain anything, least of all how I understood what she did. How I didn't think it was the wrong decision.

I wasn't going to find anything here in the Protectorate's archives to scratch the itch that had been growing since the night before.

I needed to do something.

I wanted to punch ... everything. I'd even shouted at a stranger on the street for catcalling me as Julianna when I went for coffee earlier. I knew better than that. I knew to ignore it, to not force a confrontation. Plus, the paparazzi were everywhere, and I needed a picture of me unloading on a random catcalling dude like I needed a kick in the head. And in my present mental state, I couldn't be certain that I could hold back. I was justifiably worried I might snap and knock him through a wall.

Goodbye secret identity, if that happened.

My parents would be devastated.

I might get cut off. And degree or not, I was virtually unemployable.

I logged out of the work station and pushed away from the table.

"Did you find what you were looking for?"

I couldn't even put my finger on what it was I was looking for. "Close enough," I said.

He knew I was lying, and knew well enough not to push. With a nod, he returned to work as I left.

I took the elevator down to the lobby, past the big, glassed-in museum exhibits of superhero exploits from us and the teams who had occupied the Keep before us. A girl, all bright eyed and full of hope at age eight, rushed out of the gift shop holding a mini-poster of the team. She nervously asked me to sign it, which I did, distractedly. I was maybe a bit too busy looking at her parents standing watch nearby, wondering if they were good parents, wondering if this little girl was safe.

The world had cracked open beneath my feet, and I couldn't put it back together. Not yet.

"Be safe," I told the little girl. "And don't take any crap from anyone."

Parents be damned if they didn't want their daughter to hear swearing. There were worse dangers than clumsily chosen words.

I pushed through the bronze glass lobby doors to the front courtyard and felt the hot July weather enfold me like a wet blanket. I wished that the weather-themed gang Storm Front would hit town and try to rob a bank or take out a research lab or something. Anything to get a bit of air flow to clear out the mugginess. Plus, Captain Thunderpants was long overdue for an ass-kicking.

I took a few quick steps and leapt over the Keep's courtyard walls and City Hall two blocks away. I didn't realize where I was headed until two jumps later, when I landed on a rooftop in the south of downtown across from the bus station.

The Hearts gang had recruiters here. Chicken-hawks, Bantam had called them. My idea of what to look for was informed by only a few minutes of conversation on the topic with her and what was almost certainly a false impression based on bad TV and movies.

But it was something. It was all I had. And I'd be damned if I was going to let go of that slim hope. Keeping close to the edge of the roof, I pulled a miniature shotgun mike from a belt pouch and plugged the ear bud into my left ear. I pulled out a pair of compact binoculars and clipped the microphone to the underside. With a calmness that I was having a hard time maintaining, I scanned the people below as they waited for people to get off the out of town busses.

It took me a while to figure out the layout of the brick bus station with the two peaked glass awnings along the south and west side to keep people dry while they boarded or disembarked. I'd lived in the city all my life, and had somehow never managed to spend any time at the bus station. And why would I? The Vanderkamps were not bus people. Even as Velvet, my pursuit of criminals hadn't ever brought me here. It was somewhat disconcerting, perched above, watching like some sort of judgmental angel.

The people down below, young and old, man and woman alike, they were the people I did this for, the people I put on this costume to protect. But I realized, standing up there in the sticky July heat, that I didn't really know them. I'd never taken the time. Julianna Vanderkamp had her elite social circles and party scene, and as Velvet, I mostly associated with other heroes and the criminals we tried to bring to justice.

For the most part, the heroes of the Protectorate were not exactly working class. Most came from money like myself, or were self-made millionaires. The only exceptions were the teleporter Gallows and the biologist Worm Queen, but they were hardly a representative cross section of the population. And there was Mister Grey, of course, but as a dead man, he had no real need for money and mostly just haunted the Keep.

Maybe that was part of why I couldn't get Bantam out of my head. She seemed to have a connection to the streets, to the ordinary people who were affected by crime on a personal level, that I had little to no connection to. I could punch a dragon through a wall, but I had no idea what it was like to ride a bus or to have my entirely life hinge on the next paycheck. And if I was honest with myself, I didn't really *want* to experience that. But I at least wanted to understand it.

I hadn't bothered to stop and listen before. Now I had no choice but to listen, and heard more than the petty conversations about the weather and minor league baseball. I heard about needing three more dollars just to get a ticket back to Chicago. I heard about needing to see the doctor, but not having insurance to pay for the medicine the doctor prescribed last time. I heard about people who had been let down, betrayed, lost hope. There were rays of sunshine down there—the old custodial worker, who seemed to know everyone and had a compliment waiting for them as he passed, or the round little woman in the prim dress handing out pamphlets for her church, who tolerated icy silence and occasional hostility with a smile and civility.

Eventually I started to zero in on the ones who weren't talking at all. I almost wished it hadn't been so easy. I almost wished for some evidence that Bantam had been wrong. That everything was okay and the world wasn't as filthy, as depraved, as she had led me to believe.

But I barely had to wait an hour before I pegged the recruiter.

He was younger than I expected, maybe seventeen if I had to guess. Curly blonde hair, expensive red tennis shoes, a lightweight red hoodie. He waited with the patience of a statue, reading the expressions of kids getting off the bus, no one with them, no one waiting for them. He let a few get off and wander away, which threw me at first, made me wonder if I'd been wrong about him.

Then I saw him move in on a girl a few years younger than him, dark haired, pale. He chatted with her for a few minutes, asking the questions I'd been led to expect. I was about to move in before she managed to break away during a moment of distraction. He only had to wait another twenty minutes for the next girl, not much older than the first, hair just as dark but a bit longer.

"He's looking for a type," I muttered.

It was luck. No other word for it. If he's looking for a type, maybe he's trying to recruit for the Concierge. Even if he wasn't, there was still a chance he'd be able to point me in the right direction.

Below me, the two teens walked out onto the sidewalk, heading north. I stowed my gear back in its place, then jumped off the roof, landing directly behind them. Both of them yelped and spun toward me in fear. I grabbed the chicken-hawk by his spiffy hoodie, my glove curled in what I was certain was soft, ring-spun cotton. Without warning, I jumped to another rooftop two blocks away, taking him with me.

He stopped struggling by the time I set down on the tarpaper-covered roof of some light industrial building. A handful of slumbering seagulls squawked and hopped away from us.

His eyes blazed, part bravado, part fear. "I didn't do anything! You can't arrest me."

I didn't let him down. His nice red shoes dangled, kicking inches above the rooftop. He had a point. We both knew what he had been doing, but he hadn't actually been committing a crime—not one that I could see him arrested for. It didn't matter that he had been luring that girl back to his place for his own purposes. It didn't even matter that she wouldn't likely have been his first. What mattered was what I could prove, otherwise I was just harassing him. I pressed my advantage before he figured that out.

"I'm not after you," I said. "I'm after the Concierge."

His dull brown eyes glanced around the rooftop, looking for help or an escape, or maybe a witness. Wasn't anyone there but us and some gulls. "I don't know what you're talking about. This isn't some fancy hotel."

"You know what I mean. You run with the Hearts," I gambled. For all I knew, he could be an independent contractor. But the individual gangs like the Hearts were pretty good about policing their domains. If he wasn't Hearts, he couldn't risk being found out to be a freelancer. I might try and throw him to the cops, but the Hearts gang wouldn't be so nice.

"That's not against the law either," he said, but his tone suggested he wasn't quite sure about that.

"The Concierge," I repeated. "Where can I find him?"

"You don't scare me," he said.

His pupils told me otherwise, but I also realized he was even more afraid of the Concierge. I might turn him over to the police, or I might rough him up. But I wouldn't kill him. The Concierge or whoever was behind him might not be so generous.

"I don't scare you, do I?" I said. "Then how's this. Since I don't have anywhere else to look, I'll just stay on you from now on. When you're trying to recruit someone, I'll be right there. When you fall asleep at night, I'll be watching. When you wake up, I'll already be there. When you go to your secret clubhouse to explain why you haven't been able to do your job, I'll be there, too. And when your gang comes to hunt you down for bringing this trouble to their doorstep? I'm going to let it happen."

He seemed to be weighing my words, lips sealed, but eyes full of worry. If I made this little punk my project, there wasn't a damn thing he could do about it. He wouldn't be able to make himself useful to the gang, and he'd be finished. I didn't need to destroy him. They'd do it for me.

"All I want is a name and a location," I said. "No one needs to know you told me."

"Jarred Ryan," he said. "Runs a modeling agency. Office in Parkside."

I smiled and set him down on the roof gently. I smoothed out his hoodie with motherly attention. "There," I said with a smile. "That wasn't so difficult, was it?"

"What are you going to do to him?"

My smile vanished. I almost told him, then decided it would be best if he didn't know after all. I set my sights on the tall condo towers of Parkside to the north, and leaving the Hearts recruiter to fend for himself, I vaulted toward my next appointment.

CHAPTER EIGHT—BANTAM

I checked my watch again and tried to conceal my disappointment. My shift had ended forty minutes ago, and I was no longer certain how long I'd be tied up. This was somewhat complicated by what I assumed was the coffee I'd been drinking all day conspiring with the food truck bi bim bap from lunch to burn a hole through my stomach to kill me.

At least lunch had been free. I'd made a habit of checking on Mrs. O and her K-Town Express truck every week after an incident with drunk skinheads last year, and she stopped charging me for lunch. Some cops got "protection" money from criminals they shook down. For doing my job, I got home cooking from a surrogate mother who wanted me well fed and married. I appreciated the food. I'd never gotten the cooking knack.

As for finding a man to settle down with ... at least Mrs. O meant well.

"We found the fake ID card and the jumpsuit, Igor," I said in Russian to the rat-faced guy handcuffed to the interrogation chair. His nose had been broken during his arrest, and he had received only the most cursory of medical attention since then. I glanced at the one-way glass on the wall and to Detective Bronstein beyond, who had brought Igor in. I wondered where else the suspect had been beaten. Wondered how badly he had "resisted" during his arrest. It was no secret that Bronstein, a senior detective and a former college baseball washout from Texas, had a mixed record for peaceful arrests.

Igor had been one of three people suspected of a B&E in an office tower that netted them a hard drive full of sensitive information. It wasn't my case, but apparently Igor only spoke

Russian. Just my luck that was one of the six languages I had become fluent in, seven if you counted my native English. As I understood it, the target had been an investment firm. I had no idea what was on the hard drive, but I didn't care. I just needed to find out if Igor knew where it was. Or, barring that, the names of his associates.

Thus far, he had been reluctant to cooperate. I suspect having his nose broken because he didn't speak English might have been a factor.

I took my most sympathetic tone. It was easier playing "good cop" when a hothead like Bronstein gave such a compelling balance. "You had your wallet on you, so we already know where you live," I said. "If you have family there, they are going to be questioned. If we find anything remotely suspicious, it is going to haunt you."

I saw a flicker of fear in his eyes. Igor wasn't a career criminal. Just a guy who saw a chance to make money and made a mistake. He was a few years older than me, mid-thirties, recent immigrant from Russia, and had likely found out that the American Dream was a lot harder to nail down than television led people to believe. He had no criminal record, but he had an air of desperation that bigger fish were quick to spot and exploit.

"Will they send me back to Russia?"

"Well, you're still a Russian citizen, so if they have an excuse, yeah, probably," I told him.

"Anything but that," he said. Tears welled up, made his eyes all glossy like a goddamned Disney cartoon. "I am not ... welcome ... back home. I came here for asylum."

Oh crap. Let this not be a complicated political situation. "Ok, Igor. I have my phone here. You tell me who your associates are, how to find them, or where they hard drive is, and I'll have them break off the search. We don't want you. We want what you helped steal. Deal?"

"Give me paper," he said. I pushed a notebook and pen across the interrogation room table and watched him write down three names and an address. "This man," he said, pointing to the first name, "He was not there with us, but he hired us. We met in his apartment at this address, maybe three times. Now. Please. Call."

I dialed Bronstein. They'd already gone through Igor's apartment and found nothing illegal. At least nothing Bronstein found. "Call off the hounds. We have what we need."

"You know I'm watching you, right?" he said. I could hear the sneer in his voice.

"Just trying to preserve some peace of mind," I said, nodding to Igor.

"Whatever you gotta tell yourself," he grunted and hung up.

I put the phone away and smoothed the front of my charcoal blazer. "So, this is what's going to happen. Two officers are going to come in and process you. You'll be held for a while until your contacts are arrested. I'll do what I can to make sure you aren't charged with anything, and if you need political asylum, make sure you talk to your lawyer."

"I don't have a lawyer," he said, a fresh panic setting in. "I can't afford a lawyer."

"You'll be provided a lawyer," I told him. *Hopefully one that either speaks Russian or has access to a translator.*

Either way, he wasn't my problem anymore. It had been a long day, and most of it had been spent assisting on other cases, which didn't bother me too much. The only open case I had at the moment was a serial vandalism case involving a graffiti artist leaving suggestive murals on the sides of downtown office towers. Maybe it made me a bad cop, but I found it was hard to get too worked up over property crimes against faceless entities like property management agencies.

On the way out of the station, I happened to run into Bronstein's partner, a young woman named Alvarez who still had that "new detective smell." A few months with Bronstein would break her in nice and quickly. I just hoped it wouldn't scare her off the force. "Hey, I just finished up with Igor," I mentioned. "You tossed his apartment, right?"

"If you can call it that," she said. "He shares a rented room in Karlsburg with another guy. They haven't been there long. Couldn't find anything incriminating."

"Two guys, one room?" I said, beginning to understand Igor's reluctance to get sent back to his home country. "One bed, I'm assuming?"

"Yeah," she said, giving me the stink-eye. "Real cozy. It is 2006, you know."

Great. Now I'm the one who looks like a homophobe. "Not in Russia, it isn't," I said. Mother Russia was not as tolerant of same-sex relationships as New England. I made a mental note to check in on Igor and make sure he had a lawyer that understood his circumstances. One never could tell with public defenders. They meant well, but there were only so many hours in the day.

The heartburn from lunch was bad enough that I couldn't wrap my head around the idea of dinner yet, so I headed straight home. If I got hungry later, there was a stockpile of chicken pot pies in the freezer.

It had cooled off a bit from the other day, but it was still too muggy to want to ride a bus in my work clothes. Instead, I loosened my tie and decided to walk. The fresh air would do me some good, and I could use the time to clear my head a bit. I stuck to the shady side of the street and hoofed it the twenty or so blocks home.

I'd been thinking about my encounter with Velvet the night before. Her heart was in the right place. I could tell that. But damn if she didn't remind me of a puppy. I didn't have time for a puppy.

And then I had to pause and examine what I meant by that. What did I think last night was? Was it a team-up, like Aram had suggested? Was it the tentative start of a friendship? I don't know how that would work in either case. If I tried to mete out justice at her weight class, I was heading for a body bag. And friends outside of capes required a level of trust I'm not certain I'm capable of. My life is complicated. Opening it up to someone, especially another superhero, is just a recipe for disaster.

I didn't need to be skilled in seeing the weak point of situations to know it was bound for failure.

Stick with the plan. Don't let a great set of legs and a cape distract you.

"No, Mrs. O," I said under my breath. "There's no special man in my life. And no, I don't want to meet your son's friend."

Yeah. I was doomed.

I was curious how far down the rabbit hole Velvet was willing to go, now that her eyes were opened to the scope of the sex slavery problem. When I became aware of how ingrained the problem was, it was within the context of a greater criminal corruption. It was a conscious act of will to see the individual problems. Some people couldn't see the forest for the trees; I couldn't see the trees. It was like one big cancer, metastasized to infect everything it touched. It was fed by a mentality and class structure that allowed women to be treated as less, as property. It was propped up by our advertising, by media, by blaming the victims of sexual crimes rather than the men who committed them.

Velvet could beat down an individual rapist, crush a group of human traffickers, and there would be more waiting in the wings to take their place. Fighting an enemy was one thing. Fighting an idea, a culture—that was a fight that couldn't be won.

I hadn't given up. But I had learned to be careful in picking my battles. Lately, those battles had been focused on another head of the hydra, but I was flexible. Velvet was charging into the fight at some point, and she was bound to shake things up. I just had to be ready.

My apartment building had been all sexy and modern when it had been built four decades ago, with ripple-textured concrete walls and sleek, vertical panels of glass accents in tangerine and aqua. The light fixtures in the lobby looked like glowing soap bubbles. It was the kind of building that made a Modernist shudder in ecstasy. The lobby was empty when I got in—no one there to see me open my brass mailbox door, extract the flyers and fat envelope full of coupons that got tossed immediately in the chrome trash can.

I took the elevator up to my floor, thankful that I didn't encounter any of my neighbors in the hallway. I didn't know any of them well, and that was how I liked it. My apartment was at the end of the hall near the stairwell that no one used except during fire alarms. I slipped inside without having encountered anyone.

I was greeted by blank white walls and austere furniture: a blocky sofa beneath a navy blue slipcover, a coffee table made from an iron garden gate with a slab of tempered glass on top. There was a reasonably sized flat-screen television on the opposite wall that had never known the taste of television programming. I bought it when I moved in, but never bothered with cable. I only used it to view my video or DVD collection on the rare quiet night.

To any casual visitor, it would appear like a perfectly normal living room for a perfectly normal, perhaps even boring, person. It was calculated. Not that I entertained any guests. There was enough light coming through the patio door that I left the lights off as I made my way to the single bedroom.

I slipped my jacket off and returned it to the hangar in the closet. The thin emerald green silk tie was returned to the tie rack on the inside of the closet door. The Oxford work shirt went into the hamper along with my bra, leaving me in a white tank top and slacks. I checked my watch again before taking it off as well. Almost seven-thirty. Still a few hours until sunset. Plenty of time to relax, maybe even snag a short nap.

Ignoring for the moment the seductive call of my bed, I went instead to the small shrine in the corner. I bent at the waist to light the four white candles. I bowed slightly to the Buddha on the top level of the shrine, touched my forehead. I lit a cone of lemongrass incense that I placed next to the small bowl of water on the main level. Kneeling before the shrine, I took several long breaths to center myself.

I'd let anger get the better of me recently. I knew better than to let anger guide my actions, but I also accepted that I was not the best Buddhist. I tried, but it did not come easy to me. Letting go was not something I was good at. It never had been.

I opened my eyes, focused on the photo on the shrine: my father holding my hand in Cannonade Park. It must have been cold out, but I didn't remember that day too well. I had only been five, after all. We were both bundled up in heavy coats, his bulky and black, mine a green wool coat that went to my knees. It was the only photo I had where we were both smiling.

I dug into the pocket of my slacks for the piece of Double-Bubble, felt the waxy wrapper beneath my fingertips with the unforgiving hunk of sugary gum within. I set it on the shrine next to the white porcelain bowl of water.

"A piece of gum?" Xia Lo said from behind me.

"My father liked gum," I said without surprise. I had been expecting her visit for a few days now. I was honestly surprised it took her this long. I didn't turn to look, but I could tell by the sound of her voice that she was talking through the grotesque jester-like mask. "I take it this isn't a social call?"

"You've been busy," she said.

"No rest for the wicked."

There was a lilt of laughter to her voice. "Are you wicked?"

I looked at my father, smiling into the camera, over a quarter century ago. *Such a happy face. How much blood did he already have on his hands when that picture was taken?* "Aren't we all? It's a wicked, wicked world."

"You've been interfering with the actions of people that have been given certain protections."

"Criminals," I said. "Criminals who answer to you."

"Indirectly."

"And you're here to tell me to stop."

Stop, or you'll be sent to join your father.

"It's not that difficult to understand," Harlequin said. "You need to be a net benefit to the organization or you'll be removed from the equation. Picking around the fringes? Believing somehow that you'll remain beneath notice? You aren't helping anyone."

"Tell that to the people on the other end of those transactions."

"There are other criminals in this city," Harlequin said. "Other gangs just as wicked as those you seem intent on interfering with. Gangs not controlled by someone who knows who you are—who knows who your father was."

"Other gangs did not kill my father."

I could hear the slightest hint of exasperation in her voice. "Roberta, there are very powerful people who would be just as happy if I killed you rather than have this conversation."

"And yet we're having this conversation." I knew what that meant. We both did. She could have killed me at my shrine in any number of ways and I never would have seen it coming. If she had wanted me dead, I would be dead. There was no question of it. I tensed, reminding myself that it wasn't too late.

"Yes. We're having this conversation."

I felt a brief rush of satisfaction. As much as I hated being in this position, I'd been working under the constraints of the Lo family's blackmail material. My father had worked for them his entire adult life. He'd been pulled deeper and deeper into their world, all the while trying to shield me from what was really going on. And then it was too late. He died leaving me nothing but a legacy of shame and a path of vengeance, a slow, deadly march toward redemption. My father had been a good man. Flawed, but a good man.

The Lo syndicate was responsible for what had happened to him, and bringing them down had been the one thing that got me up in the morning for as long as I could remember. The fact that I had gotten the attention of Lo's right hand meant I was having an effect. It was a far cry from bringing down a criminal dynasty, but as long as I could stay alive and look for cracks, I had a chance.

"No more attacks on the Diamonds or Clubs," I said with a nod. "Understood."

"Or the Swords or Hearts," she said.

I was taken off guard a bit. I hadn't messed with the Swords or Hearts. The Swords had bigger enemies, so I didn't even bother trying to make an impact there. And despite having built up a substantial file on the Hearts gang, I had yet to move against them. But something in Xia Lo's tone set off an alarm.

"I haven't touched the Swords or Hearts."

"Hmm."

I looked at her over my shoulder. "Hmm? What hmmm? I haven't touched the Hearts. Did someone go after the Concierge or something?"

"A recruiter," Xia Lo said. "Someone called it in right before I came here. It was close by. They snatched him off the streets. We haven't found him yet."

"I just came from work," I said. "Costume is neatly folded and put away. Anyway, I don't act before sunset. It's bad form."

She watched me like the cartoonish black eyes on her mask were staring through me. It unnerved the crap out of most people. I wasn't most people. "I believe you. But it raises other concerns."

"You know what the Hearts gang does, right?"

She looked at me like I was stupid. "What kind of question is that?"

"Just surprised how much people were able to overlook to justify a bottom line."

She was on me in two quick steps, gloved fingers pinching a nerve cluster in my shoulder. I would have likely fallen over were I not already kneeling.

"This is what happens, chicken girl," the Harlequin said. "We own you. Do as you're told, or you vanish amidst scandal and mystery. People will write folk songs about what happens to you. Do you understand?"

"Crystal clear," I answered through clenched teeth.

She held me there, transfixed. The intensity of the pain brought sparkles at the corner of my vision, and I wondered if she was doing permanent damage. "Excellent." She let me go, finally convinced. I slumped before my shrine, the pain in my shoulder retreating as quickly as it had come.

I couldn't bear to look at my father. Despite his permanent smile, I could feel him judging me for falling down the same dangerous hole he had in his youth. Maybe it was the costume. Maybe it was in our blood. Maybe our whole line was cursed to fall to corruption.

"I'm writing down an address," Xia Lo said. "You'll suit up and go there immediately. Protect the person there. They're too valuable to risk now."

I nodded, no question in my heart that I would do as directed. A silent tear rolled down to the tip of my nose before falling to splash on the shrine.

I'm sorry, Dad. We both deserved better.

CHAPTER NINE—XIA LO

She sat in the back of an armored limo, helmet staring blankly from its resting place on the leather seat beside her. The smoky peat burn of 18-year-old scotch haunted her tongue like the ghost of a wealthy alcoholic. She knew she shouldn't drink yet, but it was only a finger of scotch. It wouldn't impair her next appointment. Her metabolism was better than that, and she needed help to quiet her mind.

As much as she was loathe to admit it, Xia Lo was still shaken by the gum on the shrine.

She had been raised with a passing familiarity of Buddhism, but her upbringing had made it difficult to follow the teachings and still be faithful to her familial duties. She jokingly referred to herself as a "Christmas and Easter Buddhist," in that she was aware of holidays and observations, even if she gave spirituality little more than a token nod.

Gum on the shrine.

Tribute to a ghost—a beloved relative lost.

Xia Lo had plenty of ghosts, but none she would enshrine.

She barely remembered her childhood, the second daughter in a family that had wanted a son. From birth, she had been a burden. She could not remember her father's face, recalled nothing but the smell of him: the reek of sour sweat and stale cigarette smoke. Nothing but that and him selling her to the Woman in White when she turned six. His goodbye had been a sincere, "You are lucky to be alive. You have always been a burden."

The Woman in White was a recruiter known to desperate families in the district. She had Xia transported to a factory in Pingfang that had been converted into a school and dormitory.

Silent attendants in featureless white masks scrubbed her down, performed a full medical examination, then assigned her a room and school uniform. The next year had been a brutal regimen of academics, physical training, and combat training with eighty other children her own age. Those who could not keep up with the curriculum vanished in the night. No one asked where they went. After the first year, twenty-seven students remained to move onto the next year's education.

That was the year she killed her first person. He had been a fellow student, a bully. All the other students believed he was being groomed for something special. He was the favorite of the nameless, faceless combat instructor, and acted like it. She stabbed him with an improvised shank carved from a toothbrush, up through his lower jaw, through the soft palate and into the brain in one savagely swift move. He never saw it coming. His thick legs kicked uselessly as she lowered him to the ground. His life gushed out around her hand as she wiggled the improvised weapon inside his skull to maximize her damage.

Xia moved to the head of the class after that, but got no special favors, no affection, no rewards or praise.

At the end of her second year, the class had been reduced to only six students.

They competed in a series of non-lethal exercises and challenges before a bleacher full of people in serious suits and military uniforms. She and her five fellow graduates were introduced to their new families by way of celebration. Finally, they had found some sort of worth. Finally, Xia thought, she was no longer a burden.

Donald Lo adopted her into his family that night, made her a niece, the long-lost daughter to siblings that had probably only existed on paper. When he took her from The Factory in Pingfang, a crescent of moon shone down on her and she allowed herself a single tear. It was the first time she had seen the outside world in two years. He took her to her new home in Cobalt City.

Eight years old, and a lethal weapon against those who sought to do the Lo family harm.

She had been sold the narrative that "Uncle" Donald had rescued her. It was an easy lie to swallow at the time. At least she felt like she belonged somewhere, like someone wanted her there. But if not Donald Lo, someone else would have taken her in. The other five graduates all found placements, though she had only come across one of them since then—an assassin for a cult that worshiped the nuclear bomb and had more money than sense.

She remembered the original Bantam with more fondness than she cared to admit. To most of the Lo syndicate, she was not a young girl. She was a weapon. But perhaps because he had a daughter of his own only a few years younger, Bantam had always treated her a little differently. Kinder, if only in small ways, though she never knew how to react, or how to appreciate it. He occasionally offered her a piece of gum, which she never accepted. She had suspected ulterior motives.

No one was kind to someone else unless they wanted something from them.

She hadn't thought about the gum for years, not until she saw it on the shrine.

The driver snapped her out of her quiet contemplation. "We're here," he said, shutting the engine of the stretch limousine off. She looked out the window to a cul-de-sac of pop-up McMansions in the late stage of construction. The lawns were all bare dirt covered over with a crisscross of footprints and tire tracks. Construction was done for the day, but there were still four people gathered around the back of a fifteen-foot box truck advertising a local lumber company with a beaver in overalls saying "Got wood? Shop McClendon's!"

A yellow Range Rover with the expedition pack roof storage system pulled to a stop in the middle of the cul-de-sac, about ten feet from Xia's car. She recognized it from the fleet of vehicles that Monica ran for the high-ranking members of the Swords. Her Jack, a broad-shouldered white guy named Josh, with Buddy Holly glasses and a Calgary Flames hockey jersey, got out of the back seat with another piece of muscle that had been sitting next to him. The two in the front seat stayed where they were, hands on guns, Xia figured. After their last interrupted dealing, they weren't taking any chances.

That was why Xia was there, anyway. If someone from the cape and cowl set tried to stop another big arms deal, it would be a good idea to level the playing field a bit. She felt relatively confident that wouldn't happen, though. The sun was still out, and they were in the quietest suburban nook in Morriston, the city's quietest suburban neighborhood. No one expected sheer villainy in the fullness of day here. Unless a group of squirrels decided to jack shit up, she couldn't imagine a problem.

She watched the guys near the lumber truck roll up the cargo door, and their apparent head representative climbed inside the truck with Josh to inspect the crates of merchandise. Xia watched everyone tense up during this portion of negotiations. The Swords usually dealt with different arms traders, so they didn't quite have the same established trust in play. But after several minutes, Josh and the other guy reappeared, all smiles. Josh's second waved to the Range Rover, and the guy riding shotgun got out with a gym bag loaded with cash. A quick check for any funny business on the payment end went smoothly, and Josh was handed the keys to the truck.

He'd bring it back once it had been emptied out at one of the Sword's storage locations. Knowing Josh, he'd probably fill up the tank and sweep out the back as well.

Xia waited until everyone was driving out of the construction site before she instructed the driver to take her home.

"Straight back to Forbidden Palace?"

As if there's anywhere else to go. What else is there but go home and take care of administrative work for the family? It wasn't like she had friends she could call up to meet her for a drink. There was no one to talk to about any regrets or doubts or loneliness. She almost considered having the driver drop her in The Hollows to see if she could scare up Gato Loco, maybe spar with him just on principle. It wasn't much, but it might fill the gap of human interaction she was currently lacking. But no. That would never do.

"Yes. Back to the Forbidden Palace."

Xia dialed up Uncle Donald's secure line. He answered on the second ring, the click and silence serving in lieu of any greeting.

"It's done. No hiccups," she said. The other end of the line clicked and went dead. She returned her phone to the small hip sheath. She leaned her head back on the soft leather seat and closed her eyes, hoping they'd be stuck in traffic long enough that she could enjoy the silence.

CHAPTER TEN—VELVET

I hadn't expected Jarred Ryan to be at work as late as he was. I knew that for someone who set his own hours, it could have gone either way. But in my admittedly limited experience, most modeling agencies seemed to hold fairly standard office hours. Not Ryan. I wondered if it was the more criminal aspects of his business as the Concierge that had kept him burning the midnight oil, so to speak. It was already past 8:30, and he had shown no signs of leaving.

The window of his Parkside office was one of only a few points of light from within the Gerald Smiley Building. A mid-century modern office tower, erected back when concrete was cool, it featured an unfriendly grid of dark glass staring back at me. Lord, but it was an ugly building. It was a wonder that the building codes had permitted its construction in the exclusive Parkside neighborhood. It had more in common with a parking garage than the brownstones, row homes, and sleek modern condos overlooking Parkside Boulevard three blocks west.

"Next time we get a cosmic level threat about to level the city, I'm leading them here first," I whispered under my breath as I watched the Concierge through his window.

The angle of my view was not ideal. I was too high to see very far into the room, but it was enough to see his desk. On several occasions, the person I took to be Jarred Ryan himself stepped to the window and looked out onto the street three floors below him.

He didn't look like a monster. And I was angry at myself for thinking that he should.

Jarred Ryan was had a touch of gray at his temples—just enough to draw attention to his full head of dark hair, styled and gelled into something that wouldn't look out of place on a Texas governor. He was wearing a white dress shirt with no tie, sleeves rolled up to the elbows. My instincts told me he was in his late thirties, though the search I'd run on him claimed I was short by about a decade.

He appeared to be a Cobalt City native, an only child. If his parents were still alive, they'd been scrubbed from his online footprint and public records. He'd been married once before to one of his models, an Olga Chernystian from Belarus, though that hadn't worked out. She had long since moved to Brazil after a year of marriage and continued to get regular print work.

Jarred had two brushes with the law on his record. One for driving drunk and once for disturbing the peace, though those charges had later been dropped. There was nothing about him that suggested he brokered the sale of women into long-term "relationships" except the fact that his public career was booking women into modeling gigs.

As I watched, he sat at his desk and started flipping through the pages of a big photo album. I was tempted to give in to my impatience. I wasn't much for waiting. I never had been. I needed to be doing something. Anything. I didn't even have the luxury of chatting with teammates over the communicators because I was doing this solo.

"Why couldn't he have kept normal office hours?" I said quietly to myself, more to hear my own voice. I had anchored myself beneath the ornate cornice of a building across the street with pitons and high-tension cables so that I could wait without being seen for hours if necessary. So far, I'd been there for all of ninety minutes, and I was about to explode.

I had hoped to find the office empty so I could break in and find some kind of evidence. So far, all I had was the word of some teenaged wanna-be pimp hustler who I had put the fear of God into. I was relatively confident he had given me the right guy. It was too precise to have been an improvisation.

But if I busted in and forced a confrontation, it was the word of an apparent upstanding member of the community against the word of a person in a mask. And if things got physical prior to me not finding proof, I'd be in a tougher spot.

All capes had a kind of extra-legal status. Those like Stardust who had revealed their real identities to the public were subject to lawsuits if they overstepped those very nebulous bounds. As a member of the Protectorate, my actions reflected on those of the rest of the team whether they were involved or not. The Keep was privately held through a series of trusts, but operating out of it required the blessing of the city council with mayoral approval. The overall effect was to hold us at least marginally accountable.

No one wanted a return to the lawless bad times of the mid to late 80s, with gritty, hyper-violent vigilantes roaming wild.

Rousting gang members at the bus stop was one thing. Breaking through the window of a law-abiding adult in one of the city's richer zip-codes was another matter entirely.

Bored, I focused on the photo album on the desk in front of him. It wasn't much, but a little game of "spot the model" might mitigate my fidgety instincts. I zoomed in with the mini binoculars from my belt pouch. I was not impressed. The catalogue was like a high-grade photo album, just with professional photos—some portrait style, some full body, a variety of looks for each girl ranging from haute couture to casual.

The girls were pretty enough, I guess. But not model pretty. Maybe department store circular pretty, but I had expected more.

Three pages later, I recognized the girl on the page. The dress she was wearing in the album was revealing enough I did a double-take when I got to the face. I had the binoculars stowed and the anchors removed from my perch in under a minute.

I pulled myself onto the roof with one hand and hopped to the roof across the street. The door knob of the roof access came off in my hand, an indicator that I needed to calm the hell down before I got to Jarred's office. By the time I had descended the two floors, I had ratcheted back my anger to an acceptable working level.

The brass plate next to the door read The Ryan House.

Classy.

I kicked the door out of its frame, sent it across the reception area and into the etched frosted glass wall that screened the tiny staff kitchen from the eyes of visitors. I ignored the doors to the studio to my left, and charged more or less straight ahead, through the door into Jarred Ryan's office.

I hadn't expected to be tripped as I entered the room and sent sprawling onto plush pile carpet. Nor had I expected the person who tripped me to be Bantam.

"What the hell are you doing here?"

The only answer that made sense was that she had figured out where I was going, and while I was watching from across the street, she had infiltrated the office. Maybe her presence had been why the Concierge had not left his office. I wondered if they had been waiting for me to put in an appearance.

"Jarred Ryan is under my protection," she said, squaring off in a fighting stance.

Didn't see that coming.

"Do you know who he is?"

She didn't shift her stance. Not an inch. She knew. She wasn't happy about it, but she knew. I had to wonder again how she had gotten here, and another, supremely unpleasant thought came to mind. *She knew who the Concierge was all along and she's protecting him.*

"Stand. Down!" Bantam said, her tonfa in a deceptively relaxed grip on either side of her hips.

"You know I can't," I told her as I tried to stand up.

Operative word being "tried." Before I had all my weight on my feet, she lashed out with the tonfa, hooked behind my ankle with the grip and pulled me off my feet again.

"Know that I can't let you do this," she said.

I rolled away from her and came up in a crouch, keeping her from another easy snatch at my feet. "I don't think you can stop me."

I gauged the distance between myself and Jarred Ryan and between myself and Bantam on the other side. I figured ten feet either way. Just a few quick steps for me. Once I had my hands on the Concierge, I could carry him through the window and out-distance Bantam easily. It wouldn't solve the bigger mystery of her connection, though. And I had to admit, I was more than a little curious.

First things first.

I took a quick step toward the Concierge only to have a thrown tonfa snag between my feet. I crashed to the floor. On my way down, my head clipped the substantial mass of Jarred Ryan's faux-marble and glass desk, cracking it.

Bantam couldn't out-muscle me, and my cloak protected me from any kind of normal attack. But going face first into the big desk was still enough to stun me for a few seconds. A straight-up fight with me at my peak should be no contest. She knew it as well as I did. Bantam wasn't going for my feet because she didn't want

74

to hurt me. She was smart and efficient. I hadn't given her credit for being this tactical, and it made me feel stupid for underestimating her.

She landed on my back with both feet. The force was enough to drive me to the ground from surprise more than anything else. "Stay. Down."

I braced my hands underneath myself and pushed up hard and fast enough to send her flying backward. "I don't think so."

It got Bantam off my back, sure enough. One problem put off for a few seconds.

Wouldn't you know it, that dirtbag Jarred Ryan owned a stun gun and wasn't afraid to use it.

Focused on the attacks from behind, I hadn't paid enough attention to my true target. It left my cloak snagged up on either side of my arms, which were spread wide. It left my whole torso exposed. I felt the bite of the pins in my gut only a second before the electrical charge lit me up.

In another fight, against a heavy hitter, I wouldn't have taken that kind of chance. I'd squared off against god-like beings from beyond and walked away.

And some child peddler with an over-the-counter zap gun tagged me—dropped me to my knees.

I wanted to curl up, which was the exact wrong reaction. I did let myself cry out, because there was nothing to be gained by playing tough. Not really. There wasn't anyone here to impress.

Back when I was Daddy's little girl and prime-time party girl, Daddy had insisted on self-defense classes. When I appeared to lack the focus for that kind of thing, he instead had his bodyguard pick out a stun gun for me. I only carried it when I absolutely had to, and lost it within the first few months. But I learned a few things about stun guns in the process.

The average sucker off the street could pick up a stun gun for under a hundred bucks that delivered something in the range of a million volts. Anything less than that was just a tease, just like anything with regular batteries or cheap rechargeable batteries. The key wasn't volts. The key was amps. 5 milliamps was the maximum allowable by law. Anything more than that, and you'd stop a heart. Most stun guns didn't bother with more than 1-2 milliamps.

The zapper this scat muncher was packing must have gone up to around 3, because it was everything I could do not to pass out.

If it wasn't for his smug smile and a well-founded fear of what might happen should he manage to get me unconscious, I might have given in.

That wasn't going to happen.

Not tonight.

I grabbed the cables and ripped them out of my belly with a scream they probably heard all the way in Regency Heights.

Scared the crap out of the Concierge, too.

I saw his eyes flicker to somewhere over my left shoulder. I took a gamble and swept my left hand back fast. Bantam had gotten her tonfa up in time to block but my backhand powered through it to send her flying into the wall.

"We're going to have a talk, you and I," I said through gritted teeth.

Son of a bitch tried to run, so I bludgeoned him unconscious with a wall. He had used up the last of my patience, but damned if I was going to kill him.

Restraint wasn't easy, but it was necessary.

I straightened my cloak as I looked around the damaged office. This wouldn't do. Too much risk that the police were already on their way. I made sure Bantam and Ryan were unconscious, then searched the office for what I was looking for. It didn't take long before I was staring down at a familiar face in the Concierge's album. Natalie, Graham's new girlfriend from the other night, looked up from 8x10 glossies sporting a variety of looks: high-class, school girl, lingerie. I wondered which had attracted Graham. I felt sick, but I couldn't linger.

By the time the cops hit the Gerald Smiley building lobby, I was a mile away with everything I needed, including two captives.

CHAPTER ELEVEN—BANTAM

I clawed my way slowly into consciousness to the caress of a cool breeze through the hair on the back of my neck. The air carried a whiff of diesel fumes, spilled beer, and stale urine. I was propped against a low wall, and the sharp corner of brick bit into my spine at about mid-back. My hands were bound, but in front of me rather than behind, and I could tell by the clammy closeness of it that my mask was still on, which was a huge comfort. Apparently there were still some boundaries that had not been crossed.

"I heard you moan," Velvet said from nearby. "I take it you're awake now?"

No use playing sleepytime anymore, I guess.

I opened my eyes to see Velvet crouching next to an inexpertly hog-tied Jarred Ryan. We were on a rooftop on the south side of downtown, maybe a block or two from my apartment as fate would have it. There were a few stacked photo albums next to the Concierge, which I recognized in relatively short order. "I'm awake. You hit like a truck, you know."

"Yeah," she said with a smile. "A pretty truck."

I smiled back reflexively. "Yeah, a pretty truck. Any reason I'm zip tied?"

"Because I didn't want you sneaking off before we talked." Velvet said. Her tone was as casual as it had been over doughnuts the other day. She made no move to remove my bindings. "And I figured you knew how to break out of zip ties."

No point pretending I didn't know how to get free, either, I figured. The department had been using zip ties for crowds for a few years. They were cheap, disposable, and compact enough that carrying dozens of them was easy, but they were by no means a perfect solution. I rolled my wrists to make the thin plastic restraint as tight as possible, raised my hands above my head then slammed them down, snapping the plastic at the latch.

"I didn't want to be there," I said. I stayed where I was sitting. No point trying to run. She showed me the respect of keeping my mask on. She deserved answers. "Whatever else you believe, you have to believe that."

Beside her, Jarred Ryan began to stir. She flicked him in the side of the head with one finger and he went unconscious again. That kind of repeated abuse over the long term couldn't be good for his brain, but I figured Velvet knew the same thing and didn't particularly care.

"Ok," she said, returning her attention to me. "How about we start with you telling me your connection to Mr. Ryan here."

"He's the Concierge I mentioned the other night. But you already know that. He falls under the domain of the Hearts gang within the Lo cartel hierarchy."

She nodded. "Where within the Hearts gang?"

"Technically under Elsa, the Queen of Hearts, who sits under the King, Tomas. Ryan doesn't have any recruiters that answer to him directly. He supplies a wish list from clients to Elsa, and she filters the list down to the recruiters."

"And what about the Jack?"

"The Jack of Hearts is named Andros, and he's a burly, foul-tempered son of a bitch. Jacks are just enforcers. Operations, not administrative like the Queen. If someone steps out of line or needs correcting, the Jacks handle it."

Velvet eyed me silently for much longer than I was comfortable with. "You seem to know their org chart pretty well."

"I should hope so."

More awkward silence.

Well, here goes nothing ...

I reached up slowly and removed my mask. She'd seen the face before at Super Doughnut, but I was nobody. My face was anonymous unless you worked with me or maybe knew me from school. "My name is Roberta Pak. My friends would call me Robbie, but I don't really have a lot of those. I'm a detective with the Cobalt City Police. My father was the original Bantam, an enforcer for the Lo family."

Velvet nodded slightly, taking it all in. "That's some pedigree. So, what's your position within the Lo family?"

"I don't have one." I saw skepticism in her eyes, not that I could blame her considering the circumstances. "No, it's true. My dad was a good man who made some bad decisions. He got pulled into a situation he couldn't control, and it just got deeper and deeper until he died. Until it killed him. I dedicated my life to taking down the Lo cartel to restore his honor."

"And that's why you wear his costume," she said. "To restore his honor by doing good in his name?"

"Yes."

"But you're working with the Lo family," she said. "Protecting people like the Concierge."

"I'm not like you," I said. "I don't have powers, or the kind of bank account that lets me buy tech that's just as good as powers. I'm a single woman orphaned by a criminal father working a city job. I don't even have a car. I don't have the muscle to go after the Lo family directly. I know that. I've *always* known that. But I know a bit about how they operate because of my father. And I'm smart."

Velvet shook her head impatiently. "That's not an answer."

"It's on the way to one," I said, motioning for her to be patient. "It's not about how big you are or how hard you hit. At a certain level, nothing is without fractures. The trick is finding them and exploiting them. I started off with a chart of the Lo family's criminal empire, and started poking around the fringes of their operations to fill in the gaps. I started to test them for weaknesses. And I got caught."

"Caught? By who? The police?"

"Harlequin," I said. "The criminal underworld's worst-kept secret, Xia Lo, the right hand of Donald Lo."

Velvet visibly stiffened. She paused to check the Concierge, to make sure he was still out, before continuing. "And she didn't kill you, clearly."

"Clearly."

"She figured out who you were," Velvet said, filling in the gaps.

"And the prospect of having someone inside the CCPD was too tempting for them to pass up. So they blackmailed me. Work for the Lo family as an independent contractor of sorts or they go public with my secret. And if that happened, I'd lose everything.

My job, my name. I'd have to leave the city, change my name, and start over. You and I both know that."

Velvet stood and walked to the edge of the roof to my left. The glowing sign from across the street lit her up in blue from below. I heard the hiss of air brakes and the rumble of a bus engine. The Cobalt City bus station had a blue light-up "Welcome to Cobalt City" sign. It fit with the other landmarks I could see from my seat on the roof. I knew I could glide from my apartment from here if I needed to. I might even be able to clear some important things out and go into hiding before Velvet could track me down.

I was in dangerous territory now and I knew it. Velvet didn't have a lot of reasons to trust me. Plus, I had actively opposed her less than an hour ago. My career, my life, my revenge, it all lay in her hands. All she knew at this point was that I was corrupt, just not the depths of corruption. But I suspected that shoe would drop sooner or later. Velvet had shown a certain tenacity in asking follow-up questions thus far.

"What did you do for them?"

There we go.

"I targeted rival gangs, rival syndicates, so at least I was still stopping crime."

"While letting the Lo family go unchecked."

That stung, because yes, it was at least a little true. I had been compelled to look the other way on a few occasions. It had made me feel physically ill each time. I tried to offset it with tactical strikes against other Lo operations but that had decidedly mixed results. "Not entirely unchecked," I said. "I looked the other way, but it still gave me insight into their organization. And I used that to take other Lo operatives off the street. I've tried to balance the advantages given to the Lo family with things I can use against them."

"They're too big for you to take down. You realize that, don't you?"

I raised my chin in defiance. "Maybe. You know your new crusade is too big to win, don't you?"

"Maybe." She turned and smiled warily. "What are we going to do about that?"

"I don't know."

Her smile faltered and I felt a twinge of guilt. The windmills that she was tilting at were not my windmills, but they were windmill adjacent. I was responsible for putting her on this path, but I wasn't sure I knew the path any more than she did.

"How much trouble are you in for not being able to stop me back there?"

"A lot," I admitted. "I don't really know for sure. If Xia Lo knew that you were coming for the Concierge, I can't be certain if she had any realistic expectations that I was going to stop you. He saw me put up a good fight right before you backhanded me to Sleepy Town Junction. If I call it in, I'll get some leeway, but it will be dicey."

Velvet nodded, thinking things through. The light from below made her a study in shades of blue, and I found myself staring as she considered the options. "Go ahead and call it in now, if you can."

I whipped out my phone and tapped in the private line. There was one ring and a click with no greeting. "Got hammered by an iron fist wrapped in a velvet glove. Went down with a fight, but lost the package."

The voice on the other end was masked electronically, but the meter of her words let me know it was Xia Lo speaking. "Did she take the package with her, or did she open it there?"

"Left me sleeping and took it to go. I barely got on my feet and out before company showed up."

Velvet's nod of agreement suggested that was close enough to the actual events she had witnessed while I was still unconscious.

Xia Lo hung up, and I replaced my phone.

"I doubt she's happy about that," I said.

The bitterness in Velvet's laugh was delicious. I'd been dealing with the Lo family in my own way for ages, but the Protectorate had been butting heads with them on a whole other level the past year or two. "She can cry me a river. Now what?"

That is the question of the day isn't it? Ok. You can do this.

I pointed to the Concierge. "If you want to talk to your date there, it would be best if I'm not around for that. I assume you're sending him to the police when you're done?"

"That was the plan. I think I have enough actual evidence to at least get the district attorney interested."

"Don't count on them taking it to trial. But it's a start."

"I'll take that chance. The D.A. isn't compromised by the Lo family, is he?"

"I doubt it. But he also hates to lose a case, so the stronger you make the case the better. All the better if it's high-profile. This should fit the bill, but I don't want to sell you on false promises."

She nodded. This was not her first rodeo. It was easy to forget that, having not worked with her for long. "And at the end of the day, he's just one person."

"He might be convinced to flip on the Queen of Hearts, but that's a big fish." I sized her up. I realized I hadn't really given her enough credit the other day. She hadn't gotten overwhelmed, and she hadn't given up. Whoever this woman was, she was determined and strong. I liked her, and found myself believing that impossible things were in fact possible. "The real question is how far up do you want to take this?"

"Do you think we can chase this all the way up to Donald Lo?"

I shook my head, doubtful. "He's insulated. I don't think there's anything we can do to touch him. But we might be able to shake things up a bit."

"How so?"

"Sex trafficking, which is what drew you in to this. It led you here." I waved to take in the rooftop and the unconscious Concierge. "That's gripping. It's flashy and high profile. It's horrible and makes them want to change things. But it's not a significant part of human trafficking. Most of it's for labor. It always has been. And that's tough for people to understand. Sex sells, even when dictating our outrage. You want to make a big dent, I know how to do it."

"How?"

I closed my eyes and took a deep breath. There would be no going back from this. Given what had happened already, the chances of it being traced back to me were monumental. I'd have to figure out how to play the angles. Tough, but not impossible.

"The Hearts gang is receiving a shipment of human cargo in two days. They're arriving in cargo containers which will be hitting the Quayside docks aboard the *Caspian Star*. It's a big deal. The gang will have a significant presence there, but no supers other than their Ace, who is jacked up on low-scale cybernetics. You can count on some of the leadership being present, and they'll have crew equipped with heavy ordinance."

"Between the two of—"

"I can't," I told her. "If any of the Hearts gang gets a clear look at me and lives, word of my involvement gets back to Xia Lo and I'm done. You're not a killer, and neither am I. Can you call on your club house for help?"

"This isn't a Protectorate matter," she said, her jaw set. "We started this, you and me."

Don't do this. Don't let her guilt you into this suicide pact …

"I'll do what I can."

Fuck.

"This bastard is going to be awake before long, so you should think about taking off," she said, indicating the Concierge with a tilt of her chin. "The shipment is in two days. What time?"

I stood up and put a foot up on the roof's tin-lined coping. "They'll be unloading the container at 5pm. They'll be arriving and getting in position sometime before that, though."

"Meet me at Super Doughnut at 4:30?"

She caught me right as I was about to launch off the roof, and I almost took an ungraceful tumble. I'm smooth like that. "Wait. What?"

"It's my turn to treat. Now go. I'm going to take care of some business."

I nodded and dove off the roof, taking joy in the snap and pop of the wind beneath my glider wings. The nighttime streets of Cobalt City scrolled by beneath me, a shifting assortment of saints and sinners, devils and angels.

I had my work cut out for me in the next day or so. If I could get my head around the situation, I might be able to plot a course out. Hell, I might even be able to keep my name and my job if I was incredibly damn lucky.

"Dammit, Velvet," I muttered to an audience of no one, "You're going to get me killed."

CHAPTER TWELVE—VELVET

Things change. People change. But despite having been only minimally immersed in the social scene the last two years, I could still track down some of the regular players, the constants. In the end, it only took me two phone calls to find out where Graham was spending his time.

The Alibi Room was in Karlsburg, just up the hill from the western edge of Parkside. To get to it, you had to walk down an alley to a set of stairs down to a steel door with a murder hole in it. Speakeasy style, it was only minimally marked, with a well-publicized password required to get in. In lieu of the password, a person could simply flash their platinum card. Its high concept was to offer people a taste of the super-villain lifestyle without any actual danger. With distressed brick walls covered in layers of reproduction "Wanted" posters and $30 cocktails, it was a favorite night spot for Daddy's little rebel who wanted to play at being a tough guy.

It was no wonder Graham gravitated to the place.

Only in his case, he wasn't so much a tough guy as a sub-human bastard.

Then I remembered there had been a Cobalt City hero just after WWII called the Sub-Human, and despite his monstrous appearance, he had been, by all accounts, a supremely nice guy.

I did an orbit of the bar, ignoring the leering looks and off-hand comments, but didn't spot Graham or his crew anywhere. I had resurrected a last-season Lila Monroe dress, white satin to the ankle with a side slit that went almost to my hip and a neckline that plunged more than the stock market in the Great Depression. It was not a dress for fighting in, but not all confrontations were settled with fists. I took a seat at the bar with a good view of the door, ordered a Singapore Sling, and waited while I listened to the remixed old-school jazz that the Alibi room favored for their house music.

I took a sip while the overly groomed bartender eyed me for a reaction. The drink was good, but not $30 good. "Quite a racket you have going here," I said without irony.

"Don't I know it, sister," he smiled, waving my platinum card at me between index and middle finger. "Leave this open or close it?"

I didn't know how long I was going to be here waiting for Graham, but figured I should limit my drinking either way. I winked at him. "Close it out. If I need another, I'm sure I'll find a worthy sacrifice."

I nursed the drink, turning away offers to buy me four more and the conversations that had accompanied them. They took the rejection with degrees of maturity ranging from "No problem" to "You're not that pretty, whore." The fourth such suitor wouldn't take no for an answer.

"Why do you have to be so stuck up?" he asked, in his attempt to be persuasive. "I got you a drink. All I want to do is talk with you a while."

I fixed him with my steeliest stare, but the mix of bravado and booze blunted any impact I might have made. "I don't want your drink. And I don't want to talk to you. At all."

"Ah, why you gotta be so mean?" He reached up to touch my cheek with a crooked finger, and I locked his wrist in a vise-like grip as a response.

"And why do you have to be such a fuckstump? I said no. Take your drink and fuck off or I'll get angry."

He tried in vain to move his wrist, and I could see him getting worked up about it, but damned if I was going to let go until he got the point. He also seemed to take exception to my name calling. "Fuckstump? What's that supposed to mean?"

The bartender helpfully intruded with a saccharine sweet smile. "It means someone dumb enough to put their erect penis in a tree stump if it has a knothole small enough."

I leaned in with a wolf's smile. "Also colloquially known as 'splinterdick'."

His face twisted with the kind of rage that usually preceded a really bad decision, like starting a fistfight with a stranger in Cobalt

City. I saw the fingers on his free hand curl into a fist as he weighed whether he should swing or not.

"Hey, genius," I growled. "Super-villain bar. Not everyone in here is a piss-stained wanna be. You get my drift?"

His eyes got big and he left so quickly he left both drinks behind. The bartender dumped the one that had brought for me without my asking.

Half an hour later, Graham finally bothered to show up, haunting the doorway in an expensive black suit with narrow lapels and shoes so shiny he could bounce lasers off of them. A wolf without his pack, he was alone, which shouldn't have surprised me too much. Despite having a small circle of sycophants, Graham wasn't exactly the most likable guy. I watched him survey the room, looking for a friendly face. I made sure that I greeted him with the most sincere smile I could fake when his eyes landed on me.

I didn't like the predatory gleam I saw flash across his face when he saw me, but I hadn't sought him out because I enjoyed his company. I tilted my head sideways, to the empty bar stool—an offer he was very quick to accept.

Graham quickly ordered something off the in-house cocktail menu made with Seagram's, Cognac, soda, and maple syrup. The menu called it Moonlight in Vermont. I called it disgusting. He turned sideways on the leather-topped stool and gave me a slow, appreciative once-over. "I never figured you for the jealous sort, Jules," he said.

I arched an eyebrow and hoped the rim of my glass hid the disgust that twisted my lips. "But you figure me for one now?"

"I've never seen you in here before," he shrugged. "Either you're feeling wicked, or you came looking for me."

I shrugged slightly and set my glass back on the dark wood of the bar. "Maybe it's both."

He paused to consider, or maybe he was listening to the trumpet solo that was rolling out of the speakers at that particular moment. "You know, I can't figure you out, Jules," he said eventually. "Every time I think I have you put in a box, you jump out and I have to find another box."

"I don't care for being boxed in."

"One week you're a slutty party girl—"

"Excuse me?"

He had the indignity to look surprised I called him out on his choice of words. "Jules, we went to a lot of the same parties. I lost track of all the people I saw you kiss and cozy up with. Boys *and* girls. You were kind of indiscriminate."

"Oh, I discriminated," I said. "For instance, you weren't one of those people I was friendly with."

"No," he turned his attention to his drink and took a long sip, biding time. "No, you weren't. You made it relatively clear that you didn't like me. But here you are."

"Here I am."

He nodded, pursed his lips in confirmation that yes, here I was. "It's because of Natalie, isn't it?"

It was my turn to be surprised, but I had plenty of practice being nonchalant. "Oh?"

His voice was crisp, eyes narrowed and hard. "She's mine. You can't have her."

"She's ... wait ... what?"

"You're either interested in me or you're interested in her. Either you've had the world's biggest change of heart, or you have your sight set on someone else. So, which is it? Come here to try and tempt me with a little bit of your honey?"

"First off, eww," I said. "Second, you talk like you own her or something."

He turned back toward the bar, but not before I saw the hint of a sly smile. "So?" he said finally.

"So?" I asked. "You can't own people."

"Oh, Jules." He shook his head dismissively. "Yes. Yes, you can."

I had expected something different. Denial, at least. Feigned shock or evasiveness. Maybe even just a silent rebuke and a walk away. But not this. Not shameless, guiltless, admission.

"And Natalie is mine," he reaffirmed. "She's not for sale. But if you agree to play nice, maybe I'll let you come over and share her."

I leaned in close to make sure he could hear me over the music. "You're a toad, Graham. And I knew about her already. I'm just saying you can't do that. I always knew you were a creepy shithead, but this is way too far."

His eyes narrowed again, shifting back and forth, "You knew? Did she signal you somehow? I'll show that bitch—"

"I knew no one would be that devoted to you by choice," I

said, suddenly worried about the beating Natalie would have coming should Graham suspect her of something. She had weathered enough cruelty already, there was no way I wanted to be responsible for more. "So I hired a private investigator who tracked her back to some pimp who runs a modeling agency."

He sipped on the last of his vile drink, stone faced. "I have very good lawyers, Jules. This is none of your business. You don't know her. You don't know her circumstances. You didn't give a fuck for her a week ago, so don't pretend you care about her now. Don't make it any of your business. You think I'm the only person who does this? I'm not unique. If I was unique, that pimp, as you called him, wouldn't be in business. People don't go to jail for this. Everyone just looks the other way because that's how things work. Those of us with money get what we want, no questions."

"This is my business," I said. "Because I don't need to have known Natalie a week ago to know that she's a human being. And we don't treat people like property."

He laughed and signaled the bartender for second round. "Who is this 'we' you're talking about? 'We don't treat people like property'? Well, maybe you don't. That's your choice. Go ahead and limit yourself if you want."

"They're not my limits, Graham," I said through barred teeth. "They're the law. They're the civil compact. They're basic human decency which I figure you have a very distant familiarity with."

I felt the edge of the bar crumple slightly beneath my hand. In my anger, I had gripped it harder than anticipated. I relaxed my fingers and shifted them to the side, relieved to see the visible damage was minimal, at least in this light.

If Graham had seen what I'd done to the bar, he might have been a bit worried, maybe a bit afraid. But he hadn't. Graham was fuck all for seeing what was right in front of his nose. Narcissists were like that, only able to see what they wanted. He shook his head, only peripherally acknowledging me.

"I never could figure you out, Jules," he said. "Two years ago, you would have sniffed three kinds of illicit drugs off a dead hooker's corpse, and then you have one bad trip and practically turn into a nun. You know they say that about you now? The ones who still pretend to give a shit? They think you went straight and got boring. You might as well have died, really."

I did know that, though I never would have admitted it to him.

I knew what my profile in my old social circles looked like. I remembered the invitation to brunch that had been floated at the event the other night. It had been a rescue attempt. A lifeline thrown out by the party boat to what they perceived to be a drowning woman. It was a good thing they didn't know how to recognize someone who knew how to swim, because that invitation had never come. I doubted any of my old friends cared that much. And I was surprised how easy that was to accept.

"And then you roll up in here," Graham continued. "A white knight all mounted up on your cause-cycle, ready to pedal your ass all over people that you think you're so much better than."

"I don't think I'm better than you," I said "I know I am."

"You're a joke. A sad nobody looking for relevance in a scene that has passed you by."

"I'll remember you said that," I said, finishing the last of my drink. They made their Singapore Sling strong here and I was glad I only had the one. My tolerance was high, but I shuddered to think what I might have done to Graham with just a little less control.

Graham grabbed hold of my elbow as I turned to leave. He leaned in close, his breath tainted with the scents of pancakes and booze. "And Jules, just between old friends, if I see people sniffing around, I'll swallow the investment and make sure Natalie is never seen again."

I stared into his eyes and saw the sociopathic disregard for life I was more familiar seeing in garishly dressed criminals. I knew madness and resolve when I saw it. I didn't doubt for a second he already had at least one plan for how to dispose of Natalie's body. I could have broken his grip. I could have broken every bone in his wormy body, but I let him keep his hand where it was, though I fantasized swinging his body like a blanket to put out a campfire.

"You're right," I said demurely. "It's none of my business."

He released his grip with a satisfied smile.

We were done there. Graham returned to his drink, and I walked out of The Alibi Room as calmly as I could muster.

I caught a cab two blocks away on Parkside and rode quietly back to my condo. I over-tipped the driver for not trying to strike up a conversation with me on the seven-minute ride. The doorman greeted me cheerfully and I waved distractedly in return, but didn't linger to talk.

A response was forming. This wasn't a problem I could punch.

But that wasn't the only thing I could do. I had been too distracted by the decentralized nature of the problem and the faulty perception of my own limitations. I had been looking at this all wrong.

I called Gino's while still in the elevator and ordered a medium four cheese pizza with garlic crust and had them throw in a can of cola. I never kept soda in the house anymore, but something about salty pizza made me crave it, and I wanted the sugar and caffeine to keep my brain sharp.

By the time Gino's buzzed up, I had things sketched out on paper and was busy crossing off problems with possible solutions.

It had been Bantam's suggestion, but I hadn't been able to hear it at the time. Yes, the confrontation at the shipping yard tomorrow was personal, but that didn't mean I was without resources. I stared at the page of notebook paper, scrawled over with my crude chicken scratch, things circled, crossed out, connected by lines. It looked like it belonged on the kinds of conspiracy walls I was used to seeing in detective shows. But it made sense. It all made sense.

I took the Protectorate communicator from my purse and slid the rubberized earbud into place. They knew to call my cell in an emergency, but for calling home base, I always found the communicators so much more direct. "Velvet to dispatch. Who's on coms?"

"Ah, Velvet," Archon said, chipper as ever. "I didn't expect you to be checking in tonight. Things are looking quiet out there."

"I have something that's gotten a bit bigger than I can comfortably handle by myself. I don't want to commit the whole team, but can you put in a request for brief conference tomorrow? I'd like to see if I can get some volunteers to help me cover all angles."

"Absolutely," Archon said. "I'll flag the team for 10am. Main conference room?"

"Perfect. By the way, I saw on the news that you snagged Pin this afternoon! Nice collar. You were looking sharp on Channel 9."

"I look sharp on every channel," he laughed. "And thanks. We thought we were two steps behind him and almost tripped over the idiot instead. Sometimes you get lucky. Oh ... I have Wild Kat calling in. I'll see you tomorrow."

I returned the earbud to the innocuous drawstring pouch in my purse and picked up my phone. I dialed a number from memory and waited almost a full minute for it to be picked up on the other end.

"Darling," my mother cooed, "you know your father and I are on our way to bed by now. Please tell me you're not calling from jail or the hospital."

"Calling from home," I said. It felt like it had been forever since I'd called my parents from either jail or the hospital, but time passes differently for everyone. "Sorry if I woke you. Everything is fine, but I'd really like to set up a call with your lawyers tomorrow. Do you think you can arrange something around lunch time?"

"Which lawyers, dear? Brown & Bailey or Williams Associates?"

"Williams. Please. I realize its short notice—"

My mom scoffed at the thought. "Please. The amount of money they've made off of us, the least they can do is take lunch with you. I'll have their office call you with details. And I trust you'll tell your father and I what this is about this weekend? We can take the yacht out."

I smiled. It would be good weather for boating this weekend. I'd have to make sure I found the time. I missed the boat. I missed my parents more. It was a shame that despite living in the same city, I didn't see them as often as I'd like. Too much history we'd rather not discuss and too much current affairs I couldn't disclose, I suppose.

"I'd like that. I'll call in a few days and we'll set a time. Love you, Mom."

She said her goodnights and I heard Dad shout a goodnight in the background before she hung up. I expect he was almost as excited as me to take the yacht out.

For the first time in several days, I was starting to feel something that was a little bit like hope.

CHAPTER THIRTEEN—BANTAM

The pillars towered to either side of the entrance, all red lacquer and gold as the Forbidden Palace Hotel & Casino swallowed me whole. I glanced at a skinny black man in a Panama hat as he rolled a small suitcase past me to the front desk, his golden yellow Hawaiian shirt covered in red palm trees as if in subconscious reflection of the hotel's dominant color scheme. While the staff swept in to accommodate his check-in at the reception area along the right, I continued into the extravagant lair of my enemy. The casino floor beckoned, bright lights and electronic noises of the slots and crowd chatter beyond. All around, the staff hustled in rayon costumes representing some mythical China that might have existed a hundred years ago if you looked to Walt Disney for accuracy. At least the air conditioning was cranked up to sub-arctic temperatures, which I found to be a relief given the heat and mugginess outside.

Barely past the threshold, and I had already counted five security cameras. There was no way that I hadn't been noticed. The Forbidden Palace had a pretty good restaurant, with a mix of real Chinese, vegetarian, and the stuff most people thought of as real Chinese food. It was a hell of a step up from the more predominant steam-table places in the city that had your choice of five dishes with rice or noodles, and which had hamburgers and fries on the same menu.

I had many fond memories of my dad bringing me here when I was little. He'd stuff me full of dumplings then leave me in front of the 50 gallon fish tank to watch the silvery goby fish scuttle around the coral while bubble eye goldfish made kissing faces. As I grew older, I realized he was doing his business while I entertained myself with the fish. Older still, and I began to wonder what kind of business he did. Career day at school was for other dads, not mine.

I went into the restaurant and was seated immediately. I set my Friends of the Library canvas tote bag on the booth next to me and patted it for some kind of reassurance. There was no such reassurance coming. I was a few hundred feet from blackjack, poker, roulette, craps tables, and somewhere in the neighborhood of 2,000 slot machines, but sitting next to me was the biggest goddamned gamble in the building.

When the waiter showed up, I ordered some dumplings for old time's sake, and ma po tofu with steamed rice. I placed a bet with myself over which would arrive at my table first—Xia Lo or dinner. She slid into the booth across from me between the dumplings and entrée, so I called it a tie and wordlessly offered her some tea.

She nodded and I poured her a cup.

"I am not often surprised," she said after a sip, "but you have managed to do so. I didn't expect to see you seeking us out."

I smiled, speared one of the fried dumplings on a chopstick and motioned to the plate for her to join me. She declined. I guess hospitality only goes so far. "Is that what I'm doing? I notice you're not bothering with the formality of your—let's call it your uniform."

"Well, appearances must be maintained," she said with a smile. "And we both already know you know who I am. Why bother with theatrics?"

"Why indeed?" I answered, willfully overlooking her theatrical appearance at my shrine the other night.

"The Queen of Hearts was most displeased with your failure," Xia told me. "I'm told that Mr. Ryan may even be held for trial."

"That is because Mr. Ryan is a criminal," I said. I took a bite of the dumpling and found them not as good as I remembered. Fucking nostalgia never measures up. "That happens to criminals."

"I am also told that you put up quite an effort against Velvet before she vanquished you," she said. "In fact, that alleged criminal faulted us for not taking his security seriously. He seemed genuinely impressed that you were able to slow her down at all."

"I'm lucky she didn't turn my head into an ashtray. She hits like a truck."

Xia smiled as if reminded of her own encounters with Velvet. I wondered if they had squared off before.

"Whether or not Mr. Ryan is found guilty, we can't continue our association with him," Velvet said. "One of his greatest strengths was his anonymity, and that is now gone. Velvet managed to take an as-of-yet untold number of his files as well. We are still assessing the damage. The Queen will have to find, train, and staff a new Concierge, now."

"Well, I suppose that's one option," I said.

Xia studied me like I was an exotic bug that had just landed on her butter pecan ice cream. "Ok. You have my attention. What is the other option?"

I smiled inwardly, happy she had taken the bait even if I didn't know if the hook had snagged yet. It was still a small a victory. "Well, for one, you could ... not."

She blinked in confusion. "I'm sorry? Could not ... what?"

"Could not replace the Concierge. Not continue in that business."

"Oh."

She sat across from me silently sipping her tea. After a few minutes, the waiter arrived with a bowl laden with soft cubes of tofu mixed with spicy, ground pork. The smell hit me like a steaming, savory curtain of flavor. "I don't suppose I can interest you in some ma po tofu?"

She waved it off, then seemed to reconsider. "I couldn't."

"It's more than I can eat," I said. It was true. With the rice and dumplings, this was two, maybe three meals worth of food. And who even knew if I'd be alive that long. "You'd be doing me a favor."

"I'll have a little," she said. "No rice."

I spooned her out a portion on the small plate and slid it across the glass-topped table.

"I don't have to explain the family's decision to you," she said.

"I know," I told her, serving myself a generous portion on a bed of rice. "I wouldn't expect you to. But will you listen to my counter proposal anyway?"

She shrugged and started picking at the meal in front of her.

"You don't make money supplying terrorists," I continued.

She interrupted, jabbing at me with her chopsticks. "That's hardly the same thing."

95

"Ask the people who it affects. But no, I know it's not the same. What I'm saying is that the Lo family has looked at some revenue streams, some very lucrative revenue streams, and chosen not to pursue them. Last year, when a splinter cell of the Chinese government tried to smuggle Nicodemus Candledark out of the country to design chemical weapons for them, you gave up their location to the Protectorate."

"That's a rumor," she said, but the set of her chin told me otherwise. I'd been studying Xia Lo for a while. Since long before I was pressured into working under her. I had become adept at reading her various tells. Especially when it was a planned encounter and not a surprise visit to my apartment.

"Ok. So it's a rumor," I conceded, letting her think she had sold me the lie. "But you don't work with terrorist organizations, either in Cobalt City or abroad. It shows that you have some discretion. Some moral compass."

"Perhaps," she said. "But it's not my discretion. I take orders, just as you do."

"Perhaps," I agreed. "I'm just not as good at taking orders as others."

I let that sit between us for a while as we ate.

"The fact is, yes, you can continue to make money with a new Concierge," I said finally. "There will always be people who seek to profit off the misery of others. There will always be those who see others not as human beings, but as property. And it isn't my place to tell you otherwise. You know your business, and how to reduce it to the abstraction of numbers in a ledger."

"I'm not certain I like your tone," she said. She finished off her tea and poured herself another cup. "No. I'm absolutely certain I don't care for your tone."

"Ah." I nodded and ignored her while I continued to eat.

Xia Lo finished her second tea slowly, watching me like a complex knot, uncertain if she should untangle me or cut through me with a knife.

"If you are wondering why I'm here and what utility I might continue to provide to the Lo family, I have a few suggestions," I said, pushing away my plate finally.

"You do, do you?"

"For instance, I have this information. You are expecting a shipment tomorrow, two containers for the Hearts gang."

96

"I'm well aware," she said cautiously, her tone clear that I should not be aware of that fact.

"Velvet is also well aware." I said. "She means to stop it."

"Do you trust your source for this information?" she asked.

I nodded.

"And why would you tell me this?"

"Because I want you to trust me," I said.

She smiled. "Because if I can't trust you, what use do I have for you?"

I returned her smile. "Something like that."

"Do you know if she is coming alone or bringing the rest of the Protectorate?"

"No," I said. "My gut tells me she'll be there alone, but she could surprise me. Consider it a peace offering. I've also brought you this."

I reached into my tote bag and pulled out a manila envelope stuffed with pages I had spent hours photo-copying from my own files. I set it on the table and inched it across the glass surface to Xia Lo.

"More peace offering?" She said, reaching out to touch it but not yet bring it close.

"I'll let you be the judge."

She weighed the situation for several long moments, calculating the risks. If it were someone else handing her the package, the thick envelope might be poisoned or rigged with a bomb. It was certainly big enough to hold an explosive charge that could take out several surrounding tables and most certainly kill her if that had been my intention. But killing Xia Lo would only make me a bigger enemy of the city's most entrenched crime syndicate. It would be a Pyrrhic victory at best, and I was never big on Pyrrhic victories. I wanted to be around to enjoy my success.

Xia must have figured the same. After her lengthy pause, she slid the package the rest of the way over to her side of the table and sliced it open with a tiny blade I hadn't seen in her hand a moment prior. She removed the pages and started flipping through them, her face placid. Fifteen, maybe twenty pages later, she looked up at me. "What is this?"

"You want to continue in the human trafficking business, I figured you should know what it entails," I said. I pointed to the stack of papers and offered her a thin smile. I had been digging around the Lo family for a long time and turned up more than she might have ever expected. Buried among that information, I found the distribution trail for the Heart gang's last large shipment. I was able to track 108 of the 130 people that had been moved into slave labor within Cobalt City. Of the remaining people, thirteen had been taken from the city and nine had just vanished entirely. "That is what I could find of the last shipment. Current locations and owners. Where they came from. Their names. Not that you need names. Property doesn't have names."

Her eyes narrowed. I heard paper crinkle "What do you expect me to do with this?"

"Use it," I said standing up from the table. "Ignore it. Burn it, if you want. I don't care. I've been told not to meddle, so they're your responsibility now."

I picked up my tote bag and started for the door. The waiter saw me and headed me off near the hostess station. I smiled and pointed back to the table where Xia Lo was still seated with the empty plates and stack of documentation. "She'll be handing the check," I said on impulse. I wasn't going to ruin a good exit by pausing to have them run my credit card. And for $20? No, the Lo family could cover this one. I didn't pause long enough for him to challenge me.

A minute later, I was striding across the sunbaked asphalt of the parking lot for a bus to take me back downtown.

I didn't let myself relax until I had crossed the bridge, the neon lights of Casino Row a blur of color behind me.

I had seen it. It was there in her eyes as I stood up. She'd swallowed the bait whole. All I could do now was pray that the hook stuck.

☐

CHAPTER FOURTEEN—XIA LO

The tea had long since gone cold. The restaurant was starting to fill up with clientele when Xia finished looking through the stack of documentation Roberta Pak had left her. She was reminded that the woman was more than just a vigilante with an axe to grind. She was also a cop, and a good one. The depth of information she had managed collect was, if not quite damning, at least incredibly impressive.

The District Attorney might not know what to do with it. The files required a working knowledge of the Lo family involvement to make sense of everything. Or a big wall covered with tacks and yarn to draw it together. The files lacked the connective tissue to be of use in a criminal prosecution. They were just bullet points.

Xia shifted uncomfortably in her seat.

This had not been given to her without purpose. Just as the information that Velvet knew about tomorrow's shipment had been given for a purpose.

She would be a fool not to be suspicious of both so-called gifts. And Xia Lo had never considered herself a fool. So what was the intended purpose of the thick sheaf of papers that sat on the table in front of her?

Had it been an attempt to evoke some sense of guilt? She had nothing to feel guilty about. She coordinated the Crime Kings on behalf of her uncle, and had come into a long established situation. "A stone does not determine the course of the river," she said to herself under her breath. The busboy looked up from the dishes he had been clearing from her table and she waved him off, distracted.

She returned the pages to the large envelope that she had suspected of being a bomb only half an hour earlier. She consulted the calendar on her phone and saw the only thing on her agenda for the evening was a data heist from Willow Banks Financial. A quiet night.

Taking the thick envelope with her, she keyed through two security doors and down one floor to the heart of the Forbidden Palace. All casinos had a place like this: a secure vault for the money, a bank of monitors watching the hundreds of camera feeds from all over the building, people with guns overseeing the security of everyone involved. The Forbidden Palace security station was unique in that it also hosted the ready-room for Harlequin.

Roberta hadn't been able to track all 130 people. Five of the people she had no record of had ended up here, sharp eyes trained on screens, looking for cheats or guns. One of them had been tasked with maintaining the Harlequin arsenal. Xia had never questioned it. Had not even bothered to learn any of their names.

Their employment—no, so much more than simple employment—was dependent upon job performance as dictated by the casino manager. One of the monitor personnel had been removed for a few weeks last year, she remembered. Xia couldn't remember if she had ever heard a reason why. One day he had been there, and then gone for two weeks, only to return with fading bruises and a haunted look in his eyes. No explanation given. None needed.

She stepped into the small, circular changing room. The sterile steel walls and glowing, white ceiling made the costume on the clear-acrylic framework look like some kind of sci-fi museum exhibit. All it needed was a brass plaque reading "Harlequin: Killer, Thief, Favorite Niece—operational from 1981-2006"

She stripped naked, carefully hanging her dress in a discreet locker. The underwear and shoes went into a drawer beneath, from which she extracted a white Lycra leotard, like a French-cut one-piece swimsuit. She pulled the neoprene leggings up over her muscular legs and followed suit with the neoprene top--one leg and arm white, the others jet black. Next came the knee-high forest green leather boots, which latched securely closed around the top of her calves. The lightly armored vest impregnated with circuitry was next, decorated with red and green diamonds the size of her hand, with heavy snaps down the left breast to seal it closed. The gloves came last, a dark green that matched her boots, with wide cuffs that fell halfway up her forearm.

Xia lifted the oversized joker head from the clear acrylic post and stared into the large, black lenses of its eyes. "Just you and me."

The large, smiling mouth said nothing in return.

She pulled the helmet on and strapped it snug beneath her chin. "Op one," she said into the internal mic. "Status?"

"We see you," came the neutral, male voice.

She toggled on the suit with a switch just beneath the jaw of her helmet.

"And now you're a ghost," said the same, bored voice.

Her eyes fell on the thick envelope. "Op two," she said. The helmet switched channels on the command. "Start the car. I'm on my way down."

Xia took her white, ceramic-coated staff from its home at the base of the costume stand. With a click, she separated it into the three folding sections and put the collapsed weapon in the sheath across her back. She picked up the file she'd been given on the way out of the locker area.

Two more security doors, the second one keyed to her biometric signature alone, and she was in the secure administrative garage beneath the casino where the armored limousine was waiting for her, engine running, door open.

She set the thick envelope on the soft leather seat next to her, gloved fingertips resting lightly upon the tan paper.

"Where to?"

"Adams and Twenty-First, the Federation parking lot, top floor."

The driver pulled out without further discussion. It was two blocks to Willow Banks Financial from there, but she had learned not to be too obvious about her activities. There were heroes in the city who would stake out her limo as a matter of course should they spot it on their periodic patrols.

She contemplated the folder next to her in silence all the way downtown as squares of light from the streetlights passed over it, one after the other after the other. She scowled within the security of her helmet, more suspicious of why it had been given to her. She was more certain that it was a trap than ever before.

The engine of the limo shut off, signaling her to action. She opened the door and stepped onto the oil-stained concrete. Without a word to her driver, Harlequin sprinted to the edge of the parking structure, vaulted across the alley, and rolled to her feet on the roof of the office building on the other side. She depressed a stud on the inside of her glove's cuff for the electrostatic actuators in the fingertips, and when she leapt to the next building over, she clung to the mirrored glass like a tree frog.

A moment's pause to make certain she wasn't noticed, and then up and across that roof. There, across the street and the roof of the apartment building across the way, she saw the sleek office tower of bronzed glass and steel that held the corporate offices of Willow Banks Financial.

She stretched out her back and arms, savoring the calm before action. It had been too long since she had been given something active to do. For an intoxicating second, she considered tripping the alarms intentionally just to give her a flood of rental cops to rough up, but knew she couldn't risk it. An alarm in a corporate high-rise, especially in downtown, could always attract a hero if it was an otherwise quiet night.

Five minutes and three gadgets later, she was standing on the stain-resistant beige carpet of Willow's CFO. The company had significant firewalls to prevent unauthorized external access. It was only after breaking through those earlier in the week that her uncle's data retrieval team realized the sensitive information they wanted was kept in an isolated internal server with no outside access.

It took three minutes to find the server, and another six to download the information onto a thumb drive. A secondary program was launched to degrade their data enough that the theft wouldn't be detected for days. With the electronics blocking she had ingrained in her suit, no security camera would have a record of her visit, and security's floor-by-floor rounds wouldn't be through for another hour. In and out like a ghost. A perfect crime.

Harlequin rounded the corner on her way to the disabled vent fan she had used to enter and almost tripped over a vacuum cleaner that hadn't been there before. She recovered from her slight stumble and found herself toe-to-toe with a hard-faced woman with precise eyebrows and long brown hair pulled back and knotted into a severe bun. She wore an all-but shapeless putty gray dress with a white collar and a breast patch reading "Trunt Building Services."

So, a less than perfect crime. But this wasn't the first time some innocent bystander had interrupted her in her duties. There were a few reactions Xia was accustomed to in situations such as this. Fright was the most frequent, followed by pleading, followed in turn with stunned silence, as if hoping she'd think they were an evolved fern and pass them by. This woman broke the curve by screaming angrily and swinging at her with a clenched fist.

Xia stepped clear from the swinging fists, though none of the swings had posed any real danger. She depressed a stud on her staff and heard the soft "Pfff" of invisible gas discharge from a port near the heavy, ceramic coated tip. The mask filtered out the gas, but the cleaning woman was not so lucky. She fell over hard mid-swing, fast asleep by the time she toppled into her cleaning cart. Pink plastic bottles of bathroom soap bounced down the hall, joined by bundles of paper towels and a few ambitious rolls of toilet paper.

Xia didn't linger. "Op two," she said. "Pop the roof and head north on Adams. I'll meet you."

"Understood," the driver said.

Xia detoured to the stairwell at a brisk jog. A glace down the concrete shaft revealed no one on the stairs. "Op eight," she said, signaling the helmet's audio commands. "Ping."

A green crosshairs appeared on over her right field of vision. She centered it on the floor at the bottom of the stairwell. "Op eight. Descent line."

A small S-hook popped from the bottom of her staff. She looped it around the hand rail and dove into the darkness. The staff unfurled a micro-thin line behind her, slowing down on a spring-wound spool as she neared what the laser sight had calculated to be the bottom. Six feet from impact, it slowed to a stop like a bungee at its apex, then detached from the handrail up top. She fell quietly the final distance to land in a crouch as the line hissed back into her staff.

She stepped casually out into the hallway past the end of the elevator banks. Harlequin pointed the base of her staff at the corner around which the security guards sat watching their monitors. She depressed a stud on her staff to send a smoke pellet their way.

She was in at a full run when the first guard ventured into the cloud of smoke. He didn't see the tiny razor she pulled from the back of her glove. The size and general shape of a plastic cocktail sword, it was drugged and weighted for throwing. The unlucky guard caught the blade with his throat from ten feet away and was well on his way to being paralyzed as she passed him in the smoke.

Harlequin reached one of the large glass windows looking out onto Adams Avenue. She set the top of her staff against the glass and pressed yet another stud. A sonic "THRUM" pulsed from the staff, blowing the entire window out into tiny squares of bronze tinted glass that rained across the sidewalk and street.

Xia ran south down the sidewalk until she saw the limo coming her direction. She detoured into the street, ran straight at the two-ton armored vehicle. She planted one foot on the bumper and another at the base of the window. A step later, she dropped through the spacious, open sunroof.

"Home?" her driver asked as he rolled casually past the building she had just plundered.

Xia took off her helmet and picked up the envelope. "Not yet." She flipped through the pages until she found the name she recognized. Trunt Building Services. They'd purchased twenty people from the last shipment. The office address was on the bottom of the page. "Take me to Morriston."

She gave him the address, then sat back to give the papers another, deeper look.

She'd been there when the last shipment had arrived, watching from the bed of a pickup truck along with two gang members armed with tripod-mounted laser cannons. They had every reason to suspect that the Protectorate would sweep in to stop the transaction, but they'd gotten lucky and transferred all the cargo out of the shipping container and into borrowed tour busses without a hitch.

Xia Lo couldn't remember the face of the woman who had attacked her at Willow Banks Financial. She couldn't remember any of the faces of the people forced into slavery on that day.

The Trunt address was on a residential lot behind a small strip mall that contained a comics and game store called Otherzone bracketed between pizza place called Gino's and Starcom Mobile store. A Cup-o-Chino outpost anchored the corner of the parking lot. It was after ten, but the comic shop was still open with mostly college-aged kids hunched over tables filled with brightly painted miniature figures. Several pairs of bespectacled eyes peered out through the front glass at the sight of the limo pulling past.

"Wait for my call at the Cup-o-Chino." With that, she tucked and rolled from the slow-moving vehicle onto the shaded suburban side street.

Until they'd reached this street, she had expected an office. Instead, she found a tract home of the generic variety that sprung up all over the suburbs after the war. It was tree shaded and centered behind a six-foot-high chain link fence woven through with slats of hard brown plastic for privacy. There was a garage poking out from the side with two vans backed into a driveway shielded on one side by the fence, on the other by a tall hedge. There were security lights mounted above the garage rigged with motion sensors, but they wouldn't pick up her suit.

Harlequin slunk down the driveway to inspect the vans. Identical. Commercial plates. Trunt Building Services painted on the side next to a stylized green figure with a mop. Between fence and van, she ran her gloved fingers down the metal links. The plastic strips did more than provide privacy. They made it difficult for a person to get a grip in the links, made climbing the fence a virtual impossibility.

The layout of these tract homes was painfully similar, at least on the surface. When she went around to the side of the building, she found the side door into the garage where she expected it to be. The lock was heavy-duty, with two dead bolts. There was a window in the door, the glass double-layered with a wire mesh between like she would expect in a high crime area.

Morriston was not a high crime area. Harlequin knew that for certain. She *was* crime.

She made short work of the door and the expensive security system on the other side. Once inside, she quietly shut the door and confirmed her suspicions about the door locks. Not twist-locks on the inside, but key locks. Without those keys, anyone inside the house was locked in.

The low-light filters in her helmet gave her a good look around the inside of the garage without turning on the overhead lights. An old wood workbench had been built into the back wall, possibly by the original homeowners. Metal shelves stacked with commercial-sized cans of food and 50-pound bags of rice and beans lined the walls, like a low-end kitchen or a survivalist pantry. Along the walls of the garage were large dog beds and plasticized cable looped through eye-rings screwed into the concrete walls. The garage smelled like bleach.

Harlequin inspected the dog beds a little more closely. The hairs on the thin mattresses were not canine. They were long and dark. Human. The bleach smell was stronger here, but it wasn't quite enough to cover the smell of urine and waste.

She crept into the house proper to stand in the dark hallway between garage and kitchen, the dark stairway down to the basement gaping on her left. The lights were on deeper into the house, and she heard the television turned down low. What she could see of the ground floor from her vantage point supported the idea of this as a simple, single family tract home. It would be where the guards and supervisors would be. It could wait.

Stepping lightly, she slipped down the stairs, thinking she was prepared for what awaited her there. Through the locked door at the bottom, she stepped into "company housing." The basement had been divided up into a prison-like dormitory with half-height walls breaking the space up into blocks. Each of the eight blocks held two cots in each where women could dream through the daytime hours beneath thin sheets. There were no windows in the room. No possibility of natural light. Through an open doorway beyond the sleeping area, Harlequin could just make out a shower room and row of toilets and sinks.

The floorboards creaked above her and she froze, listening to the sound of footsteps traversing the kitchen she had seen before entering the basement. One set of footsteps. Heavy tread. The creak of old pipes from the kitchen sink being run. Longer than just a glass of water. No, someone cooking, maybe, but in view of the one way out of the basement, at least for now.

She took the momentary setback to move among the beds, inspect the meager belongings of the people who slept there. Small tables next to the beds held photos and little curios from home. Postcards and letters. She wondered which bed belonged to the woman she had encountered at Willow Bank earlier in the evening. Found herself wondering if the incident would necessitate the manager of this house to lock her into the garage for a time, as if she needed correction for something so far out of her control as a chance encounter with Harlequin.

Harlequin straightened and looked around the sleeping quarters again. Sixteen cots. Less than half of her initial class at The Factory. But she had only been a child then. And they'd been provided real rooms. Shared with three other girls, but still rooms. Not cells.

Footsteps in the kitchen drew her eyes to the ceiling again. Within the helmet, Xia's lips were a hard, thin line.

She moved up the stairs as quietly as a ghost.

There was a man chopping onion in the kitchen with his back turned to the basement stairs. His hair was short with a touch of gray. He was reasonably well muscled beneath his navy blue tank-top, skin glistening with sweat in the July evening heat, a black stylized eagle tattoo on his shoulders writhing almost lifelike with his motion.

He picked up the cutting board to scrape the onions into a large cast-iron skillet on the stove to his right, and saw Harlequin out of the corner of his eye. He dropped the wooden cutting board with a thud. Minced onions spilled all over the faded brown linoleum. "Holy Jesus!"

Harlequin did not react, still as the grave.

"You scared the hell out of me," the cook said.

Harlequin took him to be somewhere in his late forties. His voice had the slightest tinge of New England accent that was so pervasive she was often surprised she hadn't acquired it herself. Despite the initial surprise, he didn't appear to be afraid of her so much as uncertain. He seemed more concerned with sweeping up the onion than anything she might do to him. Curious.

"If you want to see the boss, he's not here."

Wheels within wheels turned quietly behind the impassive black lenses of the Harlequin mask. "Get him here," she said, finally.

He looked up from the onions, a squint to his face like he had misheard her. "What? Now?"

She didn't answer, listening for sounds from elsewhere in the house. There were no voices. Empty beds downstairs, two vans outside. Wheels within wheels.

"Call him now. Then go fetch the others."

He didn't hesitate. There was a blank space on the wall that had once held an old phone, the jack staring at them like an empty eye. Instead, he pulled a cheap flip-phone out of his pocket and speed-dialed the boss. It rang for a while before someone answered on the other end.

"Hey, it's Mike down at the house. Put Mr. Trunt on," he said, eyes shifting up to Harlequin nervously. "Don't argue with me, Gloria. Fucking do what you're told."

He tilted the phone down to smile at Harlequin. "It's so hard to find good help these days, am I right?" She did not return the gesture, remained watching him impassively from the doorway. He snapped the mouthpiece back into place. "Mr. Trunt, sir. Um, the Harlequin is here ... yeah, at the house."

His eyes betrayed his nervousness. "She didn't say. Just told me to get you here." He nodded, the nervousness intensified and he moved the mouthpiece again. "Can I tell him what this is regarding?"

Harlequin said nothing. Did not move. Continued to stare at him with huge, soulless black eyes.

"She won't say," Mike said into the phone. He seemed to be sweating heavier than before. "Yeah, now. Ok. I'll tell her." He closed the phone and returned it to his pocket. "He'll be here in 40 minutes."

He must have read something about Harlequin's curt head nod as critical because his voice immediately took on a defensive tone.

"He needs to drive up from Regency Heights. You said something about getting the others?"

Another crisp nod and he scurried off, onions forgotten, to round up other three men in the house. Even the two who had apparently been woken up from a sleep, shirtless with mussed hair and sweatpants, had a swagger about them that spoke volumes about their character. They were hard men, used to a certain order of things—cocky, bullies who weren't used to a disruption of the social order.

"There's something I need to show you in the garage," she said, indicating the door with the tip of her staff. They hesitated, but Mike led the way and the rest followed quickly enough.

Harlequin was the last one in, blocking the doorway while the four supervisors and drivers looked around, finding nothing there for Harlequin to show them, nothing they weren't already intimately familiar with. She pointed to Mike with one end of her staff and depressed a stud. A pair or razor-edged prongs eight inches long sprang from the tip. "The wall. Now. Chain yourselves up and toss me the keys."

She saw them considering the odds, looking back and forth at each other as if in telepathic conference. Four of them, all relatively burly, against one woman with a stick. Surely they could overpower her.

Beneath the Harlequin mask, Xia Lo smiled.

CHAPTER FIFTEEN—VELVET

"Could you make it out to Lucy?" the soccer mom said, holding out a pen and bag of apple fritters for me to sign. "You're my favorite."

I smiled and scrawled it out with the boldly slashed "V" at the front of my name and handed it back to Lucy.

She lingered for a moment, a question she didn't know how to ask burning her up.

"Thank you, Lucy," I said. "Always nice to meet a fan."

"So ... about Knockabout," she ventured, leaning in for a conspiratorial whisper. "Have you two ever ... you know—"

Much to my relief, Amir rushed out from behind the counter to shoo Lucy toward the door. "Out!" He pointed to carefully hand-lettered sign next to the door that read. "No Groupies. No Excessive Fanboying." Knockabout and I had a very professional relationship, but the truth was that I wasn't his type, and he was very discreet about his romantic life. I was much happier just avoiding the question entirely.

Lucy looked back over her shoulder through the glass door, but didn't linger. She was headed for her SUV with the "Namaste" bumper sticker by the time Amir returned to his post behind the register.

"I'm sorry about that," he said, smiling nervously. "Usually our customers are more respectful."

I gave him my most reassuring smile. "It's okay. It happens." I turned my attention to the racks of doughnuts behind him that were tilted for optimum display.

I ended up selecting four of the crullers that Bantam had seemed to enjoy, plus two of those horrible cans of coffee to balance the sweetness of the doughnuts.

Amir had a knowing sparkle in his eyes as he rang me up. It made me wonder if Bantam had mentioned me on our previous visit. I thought I heard him whisper "Team up!" when he turned to get the cans of coffee from the cooler behind the counter. I paid with a crisp $20 I'd gotten out of an ATM around the corner of my building for just this occasion. It seemed I never carried cash anymore.

I stepped out into the blazing afternoon sun. I was glad I'd applied sun-blocker on my face to avoid any telling tan-lines. I gave extra attention around the eye-holes of my mask. That was a classic rookie slip-up.

A quick hop and I was at the rooftop picnic table. Bantam was already waiting for me.

"First thing first." I handed her the bag and a coffee. "Two of those doughnuts are mine, for the record. Don't bogart them."

She laughed. "Bogart? Who talks like that?"

"That's part two," I told her. I sat across from her and dropped my hood. My blonde hair cascaded out from around the back of my mask. Seconds later, I'd removed the mask, too. "So, I'm Julianna Vanderkamp. You may recognize me from tabloids or the news."

Bantam ... no, not Bantam ... Robbie stared at me for much longer than I was comfortable with. "Huh," was her only reaction.

"Did you already figure that part out?" I tried not to sound worried, brushed my concern off with a smile. It would be bad if people could figure out my secret identity in such a short period of time.

She rubbed the back of her neck, looking down at the bag of doughnuts. "No. Actually, I had consciously decided not to try and figure out the identities of other heroes. Sort of a gentleman's agreement."

"That's noble," I said, though it didn't really address my concerns.

"Sort of. But it's also safer considering my somewhat problematic relationship with the Lo family."

"I hadn't considered that."

112

I lifted my mask to my face to put back on, but she stopped me with a wave of her hand. "The cat's out of the bag already," she said. "Might as well get comfortable."

My smile was more relaxed this time. "Ok then. Hand me a doughnut."

"Speaking of dramatic reveals, Xia Lo knows you're coming," she said as casually as if she'd asked for me to pass the salt.

"How did she find out? Actually, how did you find out that she found out?"

She looked up from her cruller. "Because I told her."

"Oh." I took a few bites of cruller, barely able to enjoy the fluffy, sweet eggyness of it. "Well, this is awkward."

"The Lo gangs have taken a couple of big hits in the past few weeks," she said between bites. "They lost an arms shipment and your Mister Grey is hitting them pretty hard on the drug house front. This cargo is a big investment and a reasonably large risk under the circumstances. There is every reason in the world that Xia Lo would be there in her Harlequin capacity to make sure it went smoothly."

She had a point. I knew that Mister Grey had been harrying drug gangs in parts of the city, but I didn't realize how aggressive he had been about it. I guess not needing to sleep gave him a lot of free time to pursue personal projects. "But now she knows I'm coming," I said.

"Don't kid yourself, Princess. She would have expected someone to show up and rain on her parade. She'd know you were there as soon as you touched down and be ready to deal with you anyway no matter what. At least now you're prepared."

I blinked at her for a few seconds. It made sense, but still, I wasn't happy about it. I cocked a fiercely maintained eyebrow at her. "Princess?"

"You prefer Your Majesty?"

I caught myself smiling and squelched it but not before a bit of blush burned hot on my cheeks. "Is the fact that I'm a society girl going to be a problem?"

She batted her damn eyelashes at me. "I have no idea what you mean."

Is she flirting with me? I mean, that's not unwelcome, but sweet damn, talk about bad timing.

"I'd feel a little bit better about this if I wasn't charging into this gauntlet alone." She opened her mouth to ... I don't know. Apologize, maybe? Argue? It didn't matter. I'd made up my mind and cut her off. "But you can't be involved. Trust me. I get that. And I'm not asking for your help."

She mulled it over, finished her first cruller and opened the coffee to not so much cleanse the palate as nuke it. "Aw ... you're not going to try and ply me with a nice dinner, or at least more crullers first?"

"Not even these crullers are worth you getting killed."

That thought sobered her up a bit. But not for the reasons I had expected. "You don't think I can handle myself?"

"You damn near took me down in the modeling agency office," I said. "I'm not worried about today. I'm worried about you looking over your shoulder for the rest of your life."

"You are a softie under the bulletproof cape and metal gauntlets," she said. "Big ol' marshmallow. But you're right. And I didn't say I'd join you. I was just wondering if you'd try—if that's what this was all about." She pointed toward the bag with the bottom of her can of coffee.

"This was to say thank you," I said. "I never would have gotten this far without you."

Robbie shrugged, smiled, and tore into her second cruller. "Probably not," she said. "And I did kind of kick your ass."

"Ha! You wish."

We finished up in a peaceful silence. She balled up the greasy paper bag tossed it into the trash can with practiced ease. The empty cans followed shortly thereafter. "Julianna freaking Vanderkamp," she said as we stood to leave, an amused shake of her head as if she finally realized who I was.

I put my hand on her shoulder and looked down into her eyes. "Can I trust you with that?"

"Yeah," she said after a sincere pause. She put her hand on the top of my velvet-gloved gauntlet. "Yeah, you can trust me with that, Princess. Now get out of here. You have some people who are counting on you."

Just a few minutes later, I crouched atop the top of southern support tower of the Coogan Bridge. As I settled to wait, I realized that Robbie never revealed why she told Harlequin about me in the first place.

I had a decent view of the South Docks from my perch, and through my compact binoculars, I was able to find the cargo ship I was looking for, owned by a subsidiary of Lo Properties. The containers were being off-loaded, and as I watched, a blue, forty-foot-long steel container was lifted by the crane and swung carefully over to the center of a cleared area on the docks.

I scanned the crane operator, and saw three men at the cab, two of whom had machine pistols in their hands. They directed him toward another container and over the space of several minutes, it was painstakingly snagged by the crane and carried out toward the first. I checked my watch. Right on time.

I vaulted from the top of the bridge to the cab of the huge, orange crane. The operator was unarmed and appeared to be a union longshoreman. He screamed in shock as I landed with a clang a few feet from him. Before he could react, I tapped the gunman closest to me on the temple and leaned him across the back of the operator's seat so he didn't fall to his death. As the second gunman began to react, I reached through the cab and crushed the barrel of his gun.

"I'll be back for you and your friend," I growled before I jumped away to where the second container was just now touching down.

I landed on the top of the first container with a resounding clang that announced my arrival with authority. I crouched slightly, ready to jump again as soon as a target provided itself. I knew they'd have heavy weapons, but counted on them not wanting to damage the people in the containers. The metal was sturdy enough to stand up to pistols and automatic rifles, but so was my cape which I'd clenched tightly around myself.

My sudden appearance drew a rain of bullets from all directions, high-velocity lead rounds that would shred a compact car glanced off the high-tech weave of my midnight blue cape and cowl like raindrops in a summer storm. As the clips emptied, I did a quick count of targets.

The Heart gang had about twenty people fanned out around the containers, most of them toward the front, but with a few at a higher elevation behind me as well. The glint of sunlight on scopes alerted me to three separate snipers high on the surrounding stacks of cargo containers. Farther back there were several tour busses idling, no doubt guarded by even more men. There were two heavy pickup trucks in front of me that had 20mm chain guns mounted in the back. Those, I could not shrug off.

Harlequin was somewhere. She had to be. I had hoped she'd be out somewhere I could see her when I landed, but I wasn't that lucky. And it was unnerving that I had no idea where she was yet. If I let her sneak up on me, she could drop me faster than Bantam had. She had more gadgets than me and Stardust combined, and was one of the best martial artists in the world.

Her and me alone, if I could see her coming, I might be able to come out on top. But with the distraction of a small army and her lying in ambush, I had reason to be concerned.

Someone back near the chain guns was shouting, "Kill her! Bring me her head and you get a bonus!" The voice was male, trace of an Eastern European accent, but with the overlapping staccato sound of gunfire echoing off the steel cargo containers, it was difficult to pin the accent down precisely.

I was sent spinning to the ground by the unexpected sensation of a hot hammer slamming into my shoulder, just above my left breast. A second shot blazed through my side from behind, like a mule kick to my kidneys.

Son of a bitch.

I rolled to my side and fell limply into the relative safety provided between the two cargo containers. In the momentary calm, I noticed a ragged hole in the right side of my cowl and I began to figure out what had happened. The trajectory from the hole to my shoulder indicated a high angle. The goddamned snipers had military grade armor piercing rounds. In my quick count, I had spotted three snipers, but there just as easily could have been more out there. Through the gap between the containers, I couldn't see any snipers lining up shots, but if they had radio contact, they'd be able to watch any route out of my temporary sanctuary.

The bullet which had hit my back had been a through-and-through, and the exit wound on my abdomen was reassuringly small. I slapped a sterile trauma patch over the exit wound, over my dress. The organic adhesives worked to close up the wound while the bonded localized anesthetics killed some of the pain.

A grenade bounced down the improvised corridor toward me. I had only a few seconds to react, enough time to recognize it as a flash-bang and curl up, my face pointed the other direction. Flash-bangs weren't meant to harm the targets, just confuse and

116

disorient. Even prepared as I was, the things were damned effective. I could feel the heat from the flash, and my ears rang from the fury of the explosion.

The rear ends of the two containers were too close together to grant me an escape, but they'd made me angry. I rushed the end of corridor, imagining I heard the sounds of pursuit, though there was no way I could hear footsteps over the ringing in my ears. I shoulder-checked the container on my right with my uninjured shoulder. It scraped across the asphalt of the shipping yard with a satisfying screech, and I had enough room to move.

"Ok, you fuckers," I muttered though gritted teeth. "Game on."

With the snipers above, I knew I had to move fast and not telegraph my movements. I swept out from around the left side of the containers, zig-zagging as I hit the first of the gunmen who had arrayed out in a fan around the front of the containers. These were regular people, not superhuman, just bullies and very human criminals. I didn't want to kill anyone, but I wasn't about to go easy on them either. I clotheslined the first one, sent him to the ground with his gun clattering off away from him. I didn't slow down, and swept low to grab the calf of the next one to flip him forward onto his face as I moved past. Moving, always moving.

Deep among the Heart gang, the snipers would be reluctant to open fire, as would the heavy weapons. At least that was my hope. At some point, they'd have to realize cutting loose with everything they had was their only option. But for now I had the advantage, even though there was a fire in my side and I could feel my costume clinging to my back, slick with blood from the entry wound I hadn't been granted the time to patch. I wondered how badly I was bleeding, and how long I had before blood loss made me black out.

I plowed through the foot soldiers of the Heart gang, one blow to each of them to drop them as I moved past, like the world's most violent obstacle course. After I'd taken down enough for them to get concerned, this big, bald guy with a stylized flaming heart tattoo visible on his pale chest charged in from the side as if to take me by surprise. I'd seen his pictures before. I couldn't remember his name, but recognized him as the Ace of Hearts, the chief enforcer of the gang. *Hadn't Robbie said something about him being cybernetically enhanced?*

Ace bull rushed me off course and lifted me off my feet with his charge, much faster and stronger than I had expected from him. But the ox had left my arms free. I felt his right shoulder blade turn to powder beneath my first overhanded hammer punch. He dropped me and reeled back in pain. It gave me a clear opening to break his jaw, so I took it.

I'd been stationary for a full three seconds, more than enough time for one of the snipers to have drawn a bead on me, but nothing. I looked up to where I'd previously seen snipers, but there was no one there now.

20mm cannon rounds chewed up the asphalt at my feet, and I cartwheeled backward on instinct. Two flips, and I sighted on the nearest truck-mounted machine gun. I hopped onto the top of the cab, and then drove my fist down on the back of the chain gun as hard as I possibly could. The tripod crumpled, and the gun itself was damaged beyond repair. For good measure, I tapped the guys in the back of the truck and knocked them the hell out also. I was done with surprises for the day.

I launched myself at the other pickup truck as they turned the barrel of the machine gun in my direction. I wrapped up in my cape in time to block the deluge of large caliber bullets it spit at me. They rained down on me like fists, not powerful enough to pierce the ballistic weave of the cape, but enough to push at me like a fire hose, slowing my momentum. I landed short of my goal by a full ten feet.

Again no snipers squeezed off another shot. Nor was there any sign of Harlequin. I braced against the hail of machine gun fire. Holding the cape across my face with only my eyes exposed between wrapped arm and lowered hood, I leaned in and pushed forward. One step, then two, then three, until I was within reach of the bed of the truck.

I tucked and rolled under the tailgate, cutting off their line of sight. Down on the oil-stained asphalt, I had a clear shot at the truck's tires, so I kicked hard, taking the entire rear left wheel off the axle. The truck teetered, tossing one of the operators out onto the ground.

I reached into one of my belt pouches and pulled out a small incendiary device which I slapped on the underside of the truck. I wasn't one-hundred percent sure where the gas tank was, but I figured the explosive was probably close enough to ignite it.

I mouthed "Boom!" with an explosive hand gesture to the guy who was just now picking himself up off the asphalt. Not wasting another second, I ran back toward the arc of less heavily-armed gunmen between me and the containers. I gauged by the shouts and pounding of feet behind me when the machine gunners were clear before I triggered the blast. The boom was enough to do the job, and I threw a fire suppressant grenade into the bed of the truck to coat the area with foam. I couldn't risk a vehicle fire setting off any ammo they'd left behind in their escape.

My world was a world of pain. The machine gun hadn't broken the skin, but I was going to be covered with bruises, and the emergency wound patch had come loose from my torso. Swinging my arms as I ran hurt enough that I saw spots. I considered a look behind me to see if I was trailing blood, but didn't honestly want confirmation of my worst fears.

What little grace I had was long gone. I was operating on pure instinct and fury now, hoping it was enough to carry me though. I plowed through a knot of armed Heart gang members and sent them scattering before me like bowling pins. On the other side, I found myself staring at the open container. A landscape of terrified and exhausted brown face stared back at me, blinking in the summer sun.

Between them and me was a lean, wolf-like man in his late thirties, an expensive white suit jacket paired with tight leather pants and black v-neck tee. In my cattier party girl days, I would have called him Eurotrash. When he spoke, I recognized the accent. This was the same guy who had been shouting at them to kill me only minutes before. He had a machine pistol in his right hand, aimed back toward the wall of bodies behind him.

"Leave," he said. A simple, one word command with the confidence of someone who is used to being obeyed.

"No."

He squeezed the trigger and the bullet went over the heads of the container's occupants, ricocheting around inside until it lost momentum.

"Next time," he sneered. "I don't miss."

A voice drew my attention up to the top of the container. There stood the relaxed figure of Harlequin, the oversized jester head helmet atop the red and green diamond vest. "Why are you here?"

Well ... poop. So this is how I die.

119

"I'm here to rescue these people."

She watched me impassively, and I took a small degree of comfort in the fact that the guy I took to be the King of Hearts was just as uncomfortable as I was in her sudden appearance. He didn't seem to be the kind of guy who took orders well.

"And do what with them? Send them back home? Give them new lives here?"

She had me there. I hadn't really thought out that part. My job was to prevent crimes, and this was way out of my area. I figured the cops could figure it out, maybe the feds. It wasn't my decision.

"Anything is better than what you had planned," I said.

The King of Hearts smiled and lowered his gun a few inches. "Anything? Really?"

Harlequin dropped to the ground by the King's side and flashed her staff in an arc around her, narrowly missing the King of Hearts with one end of it. I wasn't certain what to make of the action until I saw a strained expression come over his face. Blood seeped out onto the collar of his jacket, and then a second later, his severed head fell to the ground, followed shortly by his body.

Some screaming followed. Mostly the people who had just been smuggled into the country to see their not-quite-friendly benefactor decapitated in front of them. I might have screamed for a second as well.

I squared off in a fighting stance, ready for Harlequin to come at me. I felt woozy, but I figured I could hold her off for a minute, maybe two if I was lucky.

"You convinced me," she said, snapping the staff into three pieces which she tucked into the sheath on her back. She unlocked the other container and swung its door wide as well. "Take everyone and put them on the busses located beyond the flaming pickup. There is ample space. Wait there with them, or don't. It's your choice."

I wasn't about to question her sudden change of heart. I doubted I could handle a real fight should she change it back. Harlequin stood aside and motioned for the now freed slaves to follow me. The remaining members of the Hearts gang didn't challenge us as we passed. The King was dead, the Ace out of the fight. Harlequin was the closest thing they had left to leadership, and she was giving us a pass.

There were three busses right where I saw them from the top of the container. Arrayed in front of the busses were seven gang members, men and women alike, unconscious and bound with industrial zip-ties. A sniper rifle lay on the asphalt in front of one of them.

I stepped up and nudged the discarded rifle with the toe of my boot.

A shoe scuffed the ground ahead of me, and I winced with pain as I took up a defensive stance. "Should I call an ambulance for you?" Bantam asked as she stepped around the front of a bus into view.

A certain degree of exhaustion lifted from my shoulders. "Fancy seeing you here."

"Well," she smiled and shrugged. "You made it sound so fun, how could I resist? But about the ambulance, I'm serious."

"Let's get our guests situated on the bus and informed about what's going on. I have trauma patches on my belt that will hold me until I can get to the med suite at the Keep."

"I think I can help with that," she said. She passed by me to deal with the chain of people whose only crime had been wanting a better life and trusting the wrong the people in pursuing it. I wasn't sure if they knew what we had just spared them from or not. They were rightfully afraid, uncertain. Once Bantam determined their native language and started speaking to them calmly, they relaxed.

Their tears of relief joined my own as I sat in the shade of the bus, counting the ones we'd rescued, imagining all the ones who still needed help.

CHAPTER SIXTEEN—XIA LO

Not even Donald Lo's private garden was remote enough to avoid the sound of police sirens. No part of Cobalt City was untouched by crime, and the bright lights of Casino Row had seen their share of emergency responses. But the sheer volume of sirens was a rare enough occurrence that it caused Donald to look up from his book, wondering what kind of crime required such a large response.

From across the rooftop garden, Xia watched him through the gauzy curtains, steeling herself to go this last little distance. Her entire body ached, and as she watched Uncle Donald she wanted nothing more than sleep. A week of sleep. She had two bullets still in her that would need attention before that, though. One was in the meat of her left thigh and she could feel it rubbing against the femur when she walked, but at least it has missed the artery. The other bullet had lodged in her chest, enough of its momentum sapped by her costume and her staff that it had cracked her sternum and then slid along the bone, coming to rest as a lead lump somewhere just north of her solar plexus.

There would be time for a doctor later. She couldn't risk being sedated for this final part. Pull the bandage off cleanly, one swift pull. Don't drag it out. Anyway, the bag she carried in her right hand had started to drip.

She pushed the pain away, stood up straight, and crossed the garden to the dwindling accompaniment of sirens. Her footsteps on the gravel of the path alerted Donald Lo to her approach, and he peered at her over the top of his reading glasses. He set the book on the table by his side, put the glasses atop it, and stood to greet her at the doorway.

Xia stopped at the base of the short set of stairs. She thumbed open the strap beneath her chin, and lifted the helmet from her sweat-matted hair with one smooth motion. She let it fall, the gravel crunching as it landed at her feet.

"You've been injured," Donald said. There was no concern betrayed in his voice.

Xia deflected that line of questioning, kept her intent focused. "A shipment of human cargo that arrived at the Quayside docks was intercepted this afternoon. It was our cargo ship, which I suspect the authorities will most likely end up seizing. And the cargo, two containers totaling 130 women, have been remanded to police custody. Eight of the women being transported died en route. Four of our men died and over twenty more were arrested."

"Did you find the people responsible?"

"The people responsible are being dealt with," Xia said.

Donald Lo nodded gravely. "Good." He took notice of the bag in her hand, and of the blood dripping onto the white gravel path. He indicated it with a tilt of his head.

Xia stepped closer to set the bag at his feet then took a step back. She nodded toward the bag, wordlessly.

He crouched and unknotted the nylon cord that held the bag closed. Ageless fingers wrestled the top open. The glassy eyes of Tomas stared up at him. Donald looked almost as surprised as the former leader of the Hearts gang.

"Who did this?" He looked up to see that Xia Lo had assembled her staff while he dealt with the bag.

"The Hearts gang is done," she said. "The head has been removed from the serpent. Some of the members of the gang will find other homes within Swords or maybe Diamonds. But most are either on their way to jail or dead." She smiled coldly.

The Hearts gang had numbered over one hundred people deep. Not counting Tomas, three had died at the docks—two snipers and the Ace, all of whom she had killed personally. When she appeared at Quayside bar named Romeo's that they used as a clubhouse, she'd been able to deal with around another forty gang members. The Queen had been killed first, a thrown razor that went through her left eye into her brain. Things had gotten hazy after that. The Jack had asphyxiated after she crushed his throat with the heel of her boot. By her estimate, she had killed close to half of the remaining forty. If they came at her with violence, they

124

died. If they fled, they were someone else's problem. She hadn't counted, but the worn out carpet at Romeo's was saturated with the blood of wicked men when she walked out.

Realization dawned on Donald Lo's face. His eyes went hard as flint. "You did this?"

She deflected that question as well. "The Lo family is out of the human trafficking business. We are done trading in human flesh. The outlying operations that utilize slave labor are being raided by the police. They have a very complete inventory, which was delivered anonymously last night. Names. Addresses. The Lo family is not implicated in any of these documents, and the authorities will take some time to process the people they arrest today. All roads lead to Tomas, who has been dealt with."

She wondered, briefly, if she should tell him of the death of the Trunt Building Services owner, and the slave masters under his employ. The women had been picked up, as usual, and returned home, though the drivers had been temporary, hired through a service to do the jobs of dead men. What they chose to do, seeing the doors unlocked and their tormentors dead, was up to them as far as Xia Lo was concerned.

Rage flared in Donald Lo's eyes. This was not how things were done. He had run the syndicate in this town for decades; since Lyndon Johnson was president. He had faced down threats from within his organization before and survived. He had maintained control while generations of heroes had come and gone. He had been the crime boss of the city through at least three or four different Huntsmen. Donald Lo *was* organized crime in Cobalt City. And he did not take orders.

But he was old. Resistant to change.

And as far as Xia Lo was concerned, he was on the wrong side of history.

He closed on her fast, the back of his right hand swung at her face with practiced precision.

Without breaking composure, without even blinking, Xia blocked the blow with her forearm.

This triggered another attempted slap with the left hand, this also countered smoothly.

Donald Lo launched a flurry of blows at her—not slaps this time, but closed fists blows meant to incapacitate. Temple, solar plexus, three different nerve clusters that Xia's teachers had shown her.

Each blow she blocked, her face impassive despite the aching protests of her injuries. Through it all she only gave up half a step to lead him off balance, open him to a double-palm punch that sent him skidding back onto the lacquered wood steps.

"Furthermore," she said as she straightened, "I am not your niece. You are not my uncle, nor have you ever been. And you will never touch me again."

She saw the panic on his face, though he quickly tried to mask it behind anger. He shouted at her, just another confused old man trying to hold onto the past, a world that was crumbling beneath him. "No one leaves the Lo family!"

"I'm not leaving," Xia said. "But things are going to be different. This family needs strong leadership, but it expects you to be at the head. Fine. Let them believe what they need to believe. Let that illusion maintain order in this chaos."

His eyes narrowed, looking for her angle. "Then what—"

"Respect," she said, interrupting his question, taking control of the situation. It was a position she realized she was going to have to get used to. "I demand respect. Autonomy. I do not belong to you. I work for you. With you. And you do not touch me again. Ever. We'll talk over the details at breakfast tomorrow."

"Breakfast?"

She knelt to pick up her helmet. "I'll have one egg, over easy, wheat toast, black coffee. See you at seven."

Xia walked casually back toward the elevator. She knew a doctor in Regency Heights who could be trusted and who owed her a favor. She figured she'd be back to about eighty percent by her meeting tomorrow. She wondered if Donald might try something—if he might have some sort of treachery in mind. It was always possible. But with the police coming down on the entirety of the Hearts gang right now, the last thing he would want to do is remove a buffer between himself and accountability. No, more likely he'd try and keep her around to pin that on her should the authorities get too close.

She'd have time.

And she'd be ready for him.

CHAPTER SEVENTEEN—VELVET

I had more bruises than a truck full of poorly packed peaches on a bumpy road. I couldn't let that stop me from making a few important appearances though. Especially since one of them was a cocktail party that I was hosting. Thankfully my wardrobe game was strong, and when the catering company arrived to set up, I greeted them in a billowy white silk shirt buttoned to the throat with long sleeves, and tailored black tuxedo pants. I'd my hair styled earlier in the day so I was rocking the Veronica Lake cascade of blonde hair over my shoulder. It was a relief, in my battered condition, that I could still stun without showing a lot of skin.

Usually prone to running fashionably late, my guests started showing up within fifteen minutes of the time listed on the invite. It had been a long time since I'd thrown a party, and the sudden event had piqued their curiosity. But it was more than just the old society circle. The guest list of sixty had included friends old and new, my parents (although I was surprised that my mother had managed to make it), their lawyer, and the one person I wanted to see most of all: Graham.

An hour in, and my condo was abuzz with anticipation. I worked the room, smiling and making small talk with people. At one point Vikki grabbed my arm and whispered conspiratorially into my ear, "I didn't know you knew Katherine Wilde!"

"You don't?" My eyes went wide. "Oh, we have to fix that."

I took her by the elbow and steered her toward the demure redhead with glasses and cultured English accent talking with my family lawyer. "Ms. Wilde, I simply must introduce you to my old friend Vikki."

Katherine smiled graciously, but I knew that after twenty minutes of conversation with Vikki, she'd make me pay for it later. It was nice having another under-cover socialite in the Protectorate, and I always suspected that Wild Kat enjoyed the high-roller lifestyle more than me. But Vikki could be a drain on anyone's Zen.

"Jules," Katherine said, "who is that handsome devil who just arrived?"

"That's just Graham," Vikki answered for me, though I already knew, as did Katherine. *Handsome devil* had been our keyword.

"If you'll excuse me," I said, excusing myself to head to the center of the room for my announcement. Once Graham wrapped his fingers around a cocktail, I stepped up onto the sturdy coffee table in the middle of my living room and cleared my throat loudly until all eyes were on me.

"I'd like to thank everyone who came out tonight. It's great to see your faces. But I'm sure you're wondering what the occasion is."

A few whispered theories passed through the crowd. I'd been hearing them for the last hour, and it was a trifle sad how off base they all were. The most popular theory was that I was partnering with a small-batch distillery to make signature flavored vodkas. I waited a few seconds to allow for speculation before continuing. "I invited you all here so that you'd be the first to hear about a new non-profit that I am helping to found."

Surprised muttering ripped through my living room in the wake of the announcement. It wasn't too uncommon for the society crowd to get on board with causes, but helping to found a non-profit was a bigger step than most were willing to take. Joining was easy. Starting something new took vision and dedication. Having a good lawyer didn't hurt, either.

"The purpose of the North Star Foundation will be to rescue and to provide safe haven and rehabilitation to victims of human trafficking and slavery. Initially, our focus will be regional, staring here on the Atlantic Coast, but we hope to expand our program nationally, and with carefully planning and enough support, internationally. Part of that mission is to raise awareness of the problem. Slavery is not something that went away in the 1860s. It isn't something that just happens in other countries. It is a multibillion dollar industry that is allowed to thrive below the surface, virtually unchallenged."

The vibe in the room was largely supportive, but I could see a few people looking around themselves uncomfortably. This wasn't just another exotic animal they'd never have to think about. This was people that they might see every day and overlook. There was also more than a little of the anticipated disbelief on some of the faces of my admittedly privileged guests.

"Just a few days ago, police began a crackdown on trafficking operations in Cobalt City, shutting down a building services company that depended upon forced labor of undocumented immigrants. Yesterday, they shut down a ring that was smuggling labor into our country, and our city, in large numbers. And today, we've had confirmation that police have begun to rescue a list of women who have been sold into sexual slavery. Many of them born and raised here, in this country, and forced into lives of prostitution by a combination of circumstance and an industry built to exploit their vulnerability."

Through my speech, I listened to the occasional gasp of astonishment, and voices muttering in disbelief. But here and there, I saw a building consensus and nods of encouragement. My parents had been informed since I signed the papers with their lawyers the other day, and they approved of the decision. They even threw some of their own support behind the foundation. Katherine gave me a thumbs-up on the sly, careful not to betray her cool exterior. Though her personal foundation focused on art restoration, she had promised to lend me her administrative expertise as needed. Even Vikki seemed to approve, with a broad smile and tears in her eyes.

And Graham, the man of the hour, stood frozen in place, fist around a highball glass, his smile like a razor. I could see all the ways he intended to kill Natalie when he returned home playing out across the inside of his fevered mind. After all, he had warned me. I wouldn't be surprised if there was a trusted employee at home who could lock her up until he got home, shrieking and terrified with the uncertainty of her fate. He might have even warned her of what might come in an effort to control her behavior, to make her more social, more careful to not reveal anything about herself.

Not that he would ever get the chance.

Katherine Wilde had texted Archon seconds after Graham entered the party alone. The Protectorate's resident genius had disguised himself as a member of Graham's staff and infiltrated his home already. By now he should be driving Natalie to a safe location.

Bantam had been right. I wasn't alone. I had friends, allies, and other ways to handle a problem I'd once thought too big to punch. They had been eager to volunteer after the meeting the other morning. I left them out of the rescue at the Quayside docks, but leaned on them in other ways. Some were busy assisting the police in their roundup, while others lent their aid in a longer-term way, their alter egos pledging public support and resources for the foundation.

"Part of our challenge is in changing the perception of the victims," I continued. "While some people choose to support themselves in sex work, too often that is not the case. Our culture does a poor job of differentiating and tends to look the other way, or worse, blames the victims for their situation. In cases of sexual slavery and forced prostitution, the tendency is for the police to treat the victims like criminals and the true criminals like inconvenienced bystanders. That has to stop, so we're planning to work with law enforcement and legislators to change how we deal with these crimes. And we're working to set up a social safety net to provide shelter, medical support, job training, and options for the true victims."

I noticed the front door open as a pair of uniformed police officers entered. *Right on time.*

"But the first step is to raise awareness. A media push will be starting on Monday, thanks to a generous donation from Starcom Industries and our media sponsors, Castile Publishing." *Thank you, Stardust and Huntsman.*

"In the meantime, enjoy your drinks and the snacks that Chef Mark has prepared. If you want to pledge donations or discuss other ways you can help the cause of North Star Foundation this evening, we'd love to talk with you. And I look forward to seeing you all at our first fund raiser when it's announced. Thank you."

I stepped down from the table to a smattering of applause. My mom intercepted me long enough to give me a hug, which reminded me of how badly I had been bruised by machine guns just days ago. "Your father and I are so proud of you, sweetheart."

"Thanks mom," I said, kissing her on the cheek. "Can you hold that thought for a minute? I have to go say goodbye to one of my guests before he leaves."

She nodded and I slipped away to speak with Graham. He was on his phone, but hadn't stopped glaring at me though his angry smile had faded as confusion took over. "Your calls going over to voice mail?" I asked. I smiled sympathetically. "I hate when that happens."

He angrily tucked the phone into his pants pocket. I could see worry at the corner of his eyes, and I won't lie, I got no small degree of satisfaction from it. "Jules. I wondered when I got the invite if this was going to be some kind of crazy gesture."

"And you left Natalie at home so I wouldn't get a chance to separate her, or maybe talk some sense into her," I said. "So I guess you outmaneuvered me there, Graham."

"She's a dead woman," Graham said. His smile had all the warmth of the iceberg that sank the Titanic.

"Then I guess those officers there will want to talk to you about murder," I said, indicating the approaching uniformed officers with a subtle nod of my head, "as well as false imprisonment and whatever else they want to charge you with."

"My lawyers—"

"—will be hearing from lawyers representing the North Star Foundation first thing on Monday," I said cutting him off.

"Mr. Graham Caulfield," one of the officers said. "If we could speak to you outside for a moment?"

His smile was fragile, but he managed to hold onto it all the way out the door of my condo to the penthouse elevator lobby with one of the cops. The second one took off his hat and nodded to me. "Are you Julianna Vanderkamp?"

I blinked, part in surprise that he had to ask, part in surprise that he wanted to talk to me at all. "Yes. How can I help you?"

"Do you have a few minutes to speak with one of our detectives regarding Mr. Caulfield?"

I looked past him to where Roberta Pak was waiting in the doorway, black suit, white shirt, thin garnet red tie. Her hands were in her pants pocket, pinning her jacket far enough back to expose the detective shield on her belt.

"Of course."

He waved Robbie over and she "introduced" herself as if we'd never met.

"Do you mind if we speak privately?" she asked.

"Not at all." I led her outside to the patio and closed the door behind us.

She led with "Nice place."

"Nice suit. Very David Bowie."

"He is a fashion icon." She winked and took out a small notebook and pen from the inside breast pocket of the jacket. "I had kind of hoped that Caulfield was going to put up a fight."

"The night's still young. Once he realizes he can't talk his way out of an arrest, he might do something stupid," I pointed to the notebook. I smiled at her. I hadn't expected to see her again, certainly not this soon. "Feel free to write that down."

She shifted awkwardly, which amused the hell out of me, because I'd seen her fight. She was not an awkward person in her element. But this was not her element.

"I was checking in with the task force before coming up," she said. "Between our coordinated raids and the assists from the Protectorate, the Concierge's list should be cleaned up before midnight. The other groups from the list that mysteriously showed up at the police station, like the Trunt Building Services crime scene they found the other night, are still ongoing. They found a few where the owners had already bailed, leaving the people behind, but we've also gotten a few arrests."

"And this will all lead back to Lo?"

"Doubtful," Robbie said. "There are levels of deniability. Plus, I doubt there's a DA out there that would want to take a risk on prosecuting Donald Lo. He's staying in place, but I think he's out of the trafficking game for a while at least."

I raised my eyebrow. "What makes you say that?"

Robbie reached into her pocket and pulled out a piece of hard, plastic bubble gum wrapped in wax paper. "Someone left this for me," she said.

"Okaaaaaaay?"

"It's personal," she said. "But between that, the info that got turned over to the police, what they found up in Morriston at the Trunt site, and the massacre at Romeo's in Quayside, it looks like Harlequin had a change of heart."

"We're sure the Romeo's thing was Harlequin?"

"It could have been a rival gang striking at them because they smelled blood in the water. I suspect that's what the official story is going to be anyway. But the timing, lack of surveillance footage or witnesses, and the fact that the only bodies were Hearts gang members suggests otherwise. By my count, she killed at least thirty people in the past several days. No one could prove who was inside the costume even if someone were to be suicidal enough to point the finger at Harlequin. And the general consensus at the station is that no one wants to believe one person could be responsible for that. Least of all me. But, yeah. I think she cleaned house."

"They were all bad people," I said, but it didn't make me feel any better. Thirty corpses was still thirty corpses. I couldn't be certain how I'd react next time I had to deal with her. If she was smart, she'd make herself more invisible than usual for a few months.

Robbie sighed and looked out over the twinkling city lights. "That's what I tell myself. Then I ask what will I do if it happens again and maybe the people aren't so bad? Will that be because I let it happen? I just don't know. I was a kid during Cobalt's so-called Dark Ages. Not sure if I want to see them come back."

"Do you think Harlequin shut down the Hearts on her own? Or do you suspect it was word from Donald Lo up top? I wonder why?"

Robbie Pak leaned on the railing. From up here, Parkside looked like a jewel. I'd spent too many nights up here only seeing the sparkle and not the darkness between the lights. Robbie had helped me see the whole picture, and I wasn't sure if I'd be able to see the world in quite the same way ever again. "Everything has a weak point, even people, even organizations," she said. "Especially organizations. You find the right crack, the right loose brick, you can change things overnight."

"So you did this?"

She shrugged. "I don't think I'm the right person to ask. Maybe. I gave it a nudge, at least. Maybe that's why those deaths weigh on me so much. I'm partly responsible. It was for a good cause, but I'm going to have to live with that cost. But this, what you're doing in there, that's helping on a whole other level. It's not enough to break stuff down if no one is around waiting to build things back up."

I wanted to tell her this wasn't her fault. I wanted to believe it myself. And I wanted to be able to tell myself that what I was doing with the North Star Foundation was enough, but I didn't know if anything could truly be enough. But it was a start. And it was better than doing nothing. "Someone's got to take a risk."

She looked me over out of the corner of her eye before looking back to the street with a nod. "Right. And they have to be willing to put in some work. Things don't always fall into place. Things can be messy. Complicated. Some people want the easy win and aren't willing to work for it."

I looked at her hand on my balcony railing and bit my lower lip. Before I could second guess myself, I stepped forward and put my hand over hers. I liked the way my fingers felt as they entwined with hers on the polished wood rail.

"Socialite superhero," I said, "with powers I got from an accidental overdose. My best friends include an African secret agent, a tiger-woman, a billionaire tech genius, and dead jazz musicians. Complicated is a Tuesday for me."

I could see a bit of her smile from the side. "I suppose the police might need to work with the North Star Foundation from time to time."

"It would be good to have a liaison with the police," I agreed.

"We might have to meet frequently to talk things through. Maybe over dinner."

I squeezed her hand lightly. "I'd like that."

She reversed her grip on the rail to squeeze back before extracting her hand. She took a business card out of her notebook and handed it to me. She'd already written her personal number on the back, I noticed.

"Call me if you think of anything else," she said. "Or, you know, whenever, Princess."

"By the way, I think I figured it out," I said as she turned to leave.

Robbie paused, one hand on the door. She glanced over her shoulder at me, eyebrow raised. "Figured what out?"

"Why you wear the rooster mask."

She turned fully, hip cocked, arms crossed with a bemused smile at the ready to hear my theory. "Go on."

"Chickens are important figures in folklore all over the world, but particularly across Eurasia where they are thought to bring the light and chase off evil spirits. In Vietnam, their fighting chickens are sometimes held as sacred, and in Hmong cultures, they're thought to draw out and consume evil spirits. And in Indonesia—"

"My dad was scared of chickens," she said quickly, cutting me off. "As a kid, he had an aunt with a particularly mean rooster that really took a dislike to him. Terrorized him for a few formative years. That's why he chose the rooster mask."

"That's it?"

Robbie shrugged. "Sometimes it's just that simple." She winked at me then made her exit.

I smiled and stayed out on the patio for several minutes while I watched Robbie make her way through the party to the front door. I could already hear the gossip spreading about what had happened to Graham. I hoped that he waited to put up a fight until Robbie was around. It would be satisfying for at least one of us to hit him.

With a sigh, I checked my reflection to make sure I wasn't blushing. I tucked the business card into my bra rather than the woefully inadequate pants pockets, then made my way back into the party.

I was eager to hear what people were saying about Graham. But more than that, I was eager to drum up some support for the North Star Foundation, and hopefully change some minds.

AFTERWORD

Human trafficking and sexual slavery is an ongoing problem with no easy solutions. But one thing we can do is drag it kicking and screaming into the light when possible rather than look away. The perpetrators of these crimes need to see real consequences for their activities, and the victims deserve compassion, respect, and another chance.

If you want to learn more, and do more, there are several organizations in place that you can turn to:

The Department of Health & Human Services runs a Rescue & Restore program which lists a large number of coalitions in your area. http://www.acf.hhs.gov/programs/orr/resource/about-rescue-restore

The International Rescue Committee confronts the problem on an international level and does some truly amazing work. http://www.rescue.org/fighting-human-trafficking

And Protect.org is fighting to protect children from unsafe households, helping to patch the crazy-quilt of local and state laws that empower sexual predators and create a new generation of victims and victimizers. http://www.protect.org/

I sincerely encourage you to make a donation to any of these causes or pledge your support in any way you can.

Thank you,
Nathan Crowder

ABOUT THE AUTHOR

Nathan Crowder is an ex-pat of the great American Southwest who has been living in the rain-soaked depths of Seattle for the past few decades. A writer of short horror, long fantasy, and superhero stories of all lengths, he is the creator of the shared sandbox that is Cobalt City. He is borderline obsessive about music, fringe candy, urban planning, and karaoke.

He can be found prowling the mean streets of Seattle's Greenwood neighborhood in search of comic books, coffee, or karaoke. Online, he can be found at http://nathancrowder.com/, or at 140 characters at a time on Twitter as @NateCrowder.